A Baby for Christmas

A Baby for Christmas

A Sweet Home Montana Romance

Joan Kilby

TULE
PUBLISHING

Chapter One

Christmas Eve…

SNOWFLAKES SWIRLED IN the glow of Mia Richards' headlights as she inched along Finley Road heading into Sweetheart, Montana. She'd been driving for over six hours and the digital clock on the dash read 10.05 p.m. Her knuckles were white on the steering wheel pressing into her enormous pregnant belly. Bare branches of cherry trees to her left were cloaked in thick clumps of snow. To her right, Flathead Lake was a blur of white. So much for the predicted light snowfall.

She peered through the smeary windshield for the turnoff to her sister Laney's house. Landmarks were obliterated. Houses were few and far between. Plows hadn't come through yet and aside from the monster FWD that had roared past her a few miles back no other foolhardy souls had ventured out.

Not far now, she reassured herself. Ten more minutes and she'd be sipping hot chocolate in front of a fire, listening to Christmas carols and catching up with Laney, all the worries of the trip behind her.

She winced as another Braxton-Hicks contraction squeezed like a vise. Maybe she should have taken the turnoff to Polson but she'd already made one embarrassing dash to the hospital last week with a false labor. Anyway, this Christmas was going to be hard enough—the first since Jared's death—without spending it alone. She needed to be with Laney.

Her breath eased out as the contraction released her. For a false labor it was awfully painful. But the baby wasn't due for two more weeks. It couldn't possibly be coming.

Rolling her shoulders to release the tension, she geared down at an intersection. The street sign was covered in snow. Was this the shortcut Laney had referred to in her email, the back way into town and her sister's house? Only one way to find out.

As she turned the corner, another contraction clamped her belly, making her gasp. Her hands involuntarily jerked the steering wheel and the little Honda skidded. Panicking, she hit the brakes and they locked, sending her car into a slow slide off the road. With a muffled thunk her car hit a hard object buried beneath the snow and tilted at a crazy angle in the snow-filled ditch.

For a moment Mia couldn't move or think. This couldn't be happening. Yet it was. She was leaning sideways to the right, held in place by her seat belt. Tentatively, she moved her feet and patted herself across the head and shoulders. Arms. Legs. No blood. No broken bones. The airbags hadn't even been deployed. As crashes went it had been gentle.

She put the gear shift into reverse and pressed her foot to the accelerator. The rear tire spun uselessly in the air and the front tires dug in deeper. Stuck. She cut the engine and in the sudden silence the wind howled.

Turning on the interior light, she reached for her phone and with trembling fingers punched in the speed dial for Laney. Red letters flashed across the screen. Low battery. Recharge now. *No.* The stupid game app that she hadn't even wanted, which her stupid boss had downloaded to her phone against her wishes, had sucked up all her juice.

The same boss who'd fired her two days before Christmas.

Speaking of batteries… She turned off the headlights. The dark landscape was bleak and cold and empty. Panic started to overtake her but she beat it down. Think. What should she do? Leave the car and try to find help, or stay and wait for help to come to her? She could be waiting a long time. People had been known to freeze to death in their cars. They also got lost walking in blizzards.

Another contraction caught her by surprise. She'd almost forgot about the baby. When the pain subsided she noticed a seeping warmth between her legs. Please don't be blood. Please, please, please… With a shaking hand she felt the dampness that soaked through her stretchy pants. Her fingers came away wet but not red. Thank God.

Except…it meant her waters had broken. She was in labor. *For real.*

A cold sweat broke over her. That decided it. She couldn't give birth in a two-door compact. Anyway, Laney was her birthing buddy. She refused to have this baby until she got to her sister's place. So that's what she would do, get out and walk for help. Crawl if she had to.

She wiped away the condensation on the fogged window and peered out. Up the road, maybe two or three hundred yards away in the orchard, a string of brightly colored Christmas lights outlined the roof of a large shed. In a window below burned a yellow light.

IN HIS OFFICE in the cherry packing shed, Will Starr turned up the electric space heater another notch. He tapped the pad of paper in front of him with the pen and pondered what he'd written.

New Year's resolutions:

1. Get over Katie.
2. Finish the damn house.

Two resolutions were plenty. It wasn't like either was going to be easy. They would be damn hard in fact. He was about to toss down his pen when he had a sudden thought and added a third resolution.

3.   Never fall in love again!

There, now he had something he could achieve. He pushed the pad aside and reached for the Starr Orchards' accounting file. Working on Christmas Eve wasn't his idea of a good time but this year he hadn't been able to get into the holiday spirit. Earlier he'd been at his parents' house for a traditional dinner complete with carols and mulled wine. His mom had decorated the house with holly boughs and pine cones. Fragrant cedar logs burned merrily in the river stone fireplace.

Normally he loved Christmas—the scents of cinnamon and pine and all the rituals his family had grown up with and embellished over the years made it a special time. His brothers Garret and Cody had been there as well as his half brother Alex and his new wife Emma. It should have been great. Instead he'd felt restless and lonesome, heartbroken and angry. Only a month ago he'd confidently expected that this Christmas, Katie—his on-again, off-again, longtime girlfriend—would be wearing his engagement ring.

Until she dumped him at Thanksgiving.

They'd been high school sweethearts and although Katie had spent half the intervening years working in other cities, when she'd told him she was coming back to Sweetheart to live, he made up his mind to finally ask her to set a date. It was about time. He was thirty-two and ready to settle down and have a family. His parents and their friends were always asking when they were going to marry. So he'd taken her out to a fancy dinner at the Montreau Hotel to propose. Then wham, she told him she'd fallen head over heels for a man from Marietta and was going to marry him.

Will wasn't the only person who was disappointed. His parents were devastated, especially his mom who'd been hoping for grandkids. She'd been extra solicitous tonight, giving him the biggest slice of mince pie and the chair closest to the fire, as if the warmth of the flames would make up for Katie's coldness. The last thing he wanted was anyone feeling sorry for him. So as soon after dinner as was polite he'd headed out, pleading a desire to be fresh for the morning so he could whup his brothers' asses in their annual Christmas snowshoe race.

After a couple of hours at the computer inputting orchard expenses onto a spreadsheet, the numbers had begun to dance in front of his eyes. Enough. He drained his lukewarm cup of coffee and rose, stretching his arms above his head.

A groan sounded outside. He lowered his arms and listened. There it was again. Was it the wind? An animal in distress? Then someone banged on the door to the shed and he heard a distinctly female voice cursing a blue streak.

Will hurried out of his office. The big hoppers and conveyor belts of the cherry processor were quiet and dark. A few bales of hay left over from the nativity scene his mom organized every year for the church were stacked in a corner, along with a spare shepherd mannequin who had strayed from his flock.

Pushing hard, he opened the door against the wind. A heavily pregnant woman was slumped against the doorframe. The security light shone on a tumbled mass of dark brown hair flecked with snowflakes and a heart-shaped face stretched tight with pain.

"Oh my God, are you all right?" He put an arm beneath her elbow and helped her inside. "What's the matter? Are you…are you in labor?"

"The baby is coming early," she said, her voice edgy. "I'm not ready. I want it stopped, now!" She bent over, clutching her belly, and let out an animal groan that made the hairs on his neck stand up.

Fuuuuck. "I'll go dig out my truck and take you to the hospital. Here, sit on this hay bale."

He led her to the bale and sat her down but she clutched his jacket with both hands, panic in her eyes. "Don't leave me. I mean it. If you go out that door I'll kill you with my bare hands."

"You can't give birth here." He pried her fingers loose of his clothing. They were freezing so he rubbed to warm them. "It's not sanitary. There's no bed."

The contraction passed and the tension drained from her body, leaving her with an eerie air of calm determination. "I don't want to give birth here. My sister is a midwife and my birthing buddy. We've been practicing over Skype. I can't have the baby until she's with me."

Relief flooded him. Great, she had someone to go to. "Where's your sister?"

"She lives on Sweet Street," the woman said. "My phone is out of charge. Could you call her to come and get me?"

"Sure." Will ran back to the office for his phone. "Number?" She dictated and he punched it in. While it rang he asked, "What's your name?"

"Mia. Ohhhhh." She bent double again. "Hurry!"

"I've got Mia here, she's in labor," Will said when a woman answered. "Are you her sister?"

"Yes, I'm Laney. Oh my God. Is she okay? She's not due yet. Are you her doctor?"

"No, I'm just some random guy whose shed she stumbled into. I'm on Finley Road. She wants you to come and get her."

"I'm not in Sweetheart," Laney said. "I was heading home when the storm hit and I had to turn back. I'm stuck in Butte. I tried to call her but her phone's dead."

Crap. Will glanced over at Mia. She was on all fours atop the hay bale, head bowed, lowing like a cow in agony. "I'll try to get her to the hospital in Polson."

"I've been listening to the road report for the state," Laney said. "There was an accident on Route 35—a tanker slid into oncoming traffic and both lanes are blocked. They might be cleared now but you don't want to risk getting stuck out there."

"No, that would be terrible." Almost as terrible as delivering a baby in a cherry packing shed. "We could go to Kalispell but that's an hour away."

"Our family is known for short labors," Laney said. "My mom delivered both me and Mia in less than two hours. How far apart are the contractions?"

"I haven't been timing them but maybe a minute or two."

Laney whistled. "You don't have time to go anywhere."

"I'll try to get help here," Will said. "Would you like to talk to her?"

He handed the phone to Mia and paced as he listened to Mia calmly tell her sister that she'd decided not to have the baby after all. If she did go ahead she would wait until after Christmas.

Was she crazy or was this due to hormones? Will knew nothing about childbirth other than what he'd gleaned from watching his parents' golden retriever pop out half a dozen puppies with the greatest of ease. If only he watched that reality TV show about the maternity ward. It would at least be something to go on.

"Random guy," Mia barked, handing him back his phone. "Laney wants to talk to you again."

"My name is Will," he told her but speaking into the receiver so Laney could hear, too.

"She's in transition," Laney said. "That's why she's saying weird stuff."

"Oh great," Will said, relieved. "I thought she might be, you know…" He trailed off, not wanting to use the phrase 'mentally challenged' in case he sparked another death threat.

"It means she's very close," Laney said. "If she starts pushing you've got to stop her."

"I thought pushing was what got the baby out." A bubble of panic worked its way up Will's throat. If he had to somehow pull the baby out, well there was no way.

"Listen carefully," Laney said. "I'm a midwife. I'm going to tell you exactly what to do."

"Me?" A cold sweat broke over his forehead. He could run a multimillion-dollar international business but delivering a baby? The mere thought made him feel faint. "Hang up for a minute and I'll call my mother to come down. She'll be better at this."

"You. Don't. Have. Time," Laney warned. "We can't risk losing our connection. Mia's contractions are too close together. Put a rubber sheet on the bed—"

"*You* don't understand." He kicked an empty bucket out of his way as he paced. "We're in a shed with a concrete floor. There's no rubber sheet. There's no damn bed."

"Drugs, I need drugs," Mia yelled from the hay bale. Now she was leaning her elbows on it, her butt waving in the air.

Will put his hand over the receiver. "I might be able to find a little weed my brother grew. Would that do?"

"Weed?" Mia glared at him. "I need hardcore, like an epidural."

Of course. What was he thinking?

"Hello, are you there?" Laney called him back to the phone. "Can you make a bed out of anything?"

He sucked in a deep breath, took another look at the groaning, irrational woman on the hay bale. It was down to him to stay calm. "I'll pass you back to Mia while I figure something out."

While Mia listened to her sister he assessed the situation. The shed was freezing so she couldn't give birth in here. It would have to be his office. He went there, pushed the desk against the wall and put the heater on the desk and turned it up full blast. Then he took the chair and the potted plant out and shoved the filing cabinet into the corner to make as much room as possible.

Back in the shed, Mia was panting short, shallow gasps. He grabbed a hay bale in each hand and swung them across into the office. Cutting the twine with scissors, he spread the hay thickly over the entire floor. Then he went to the store room and grabbed a couple of towels and half a dozen pairs of overalls, worn but clean. The overalls he laid over the straw. The towels he placed on the desk ready to wrap the baby in. It was pitifully inadequate but it would have to do. He shuddered to think what would have happened to her if he hadn't been here tonight. She would have been all alone, in the cold.

Unreality flashed over him. A woman was going to have a baby in his office. On a bed of hay.

Don't think. Get a grip.

"Mia, your birthing chamber is ready." Taking her arm, he led her into the office and shut the door. "Take your pants off and cover up with one of the overalls. Leave your top and coat on."

He wasn't sure where this calm, authoritative manner was coming from. Maybe he'd been a doctor in another life. Or maybe he was trying to avoid thinking about the fact that he was in charge of a situation he had no experience with, a situation that could be life-threatening to the mother or the baby or both.

If he was scared, Mia had to be terrified.

He took his phone from her and turned his back while she removed her clothing. Laney told him to check how far Mia was dilated, and how to rub her perineum to stretch the skin so she wouldn't tear. The sound of doing all that made him light-headed and he had to sit on the desk. A buzzing in his ears meant he missed half of what Laney was saying. "Can you repeat that, please?"

Finally, he had the gist. In theory, it was pretty simple...unless something went wrong.

"I'm putting you on speaker." He set the phone on the desk and kneeled beside Mia. The thick bed of hay was soft and smelled comfortingly of summer. She was propped on her elbows, her face pale and drawn. He took off his belt and handed it to her. "In case you need to bite down."

"You're not amputating my leg." Another contraction gripped her. She grabbed the belt and squeezed with both hands. "I have to push."

"Not yet. Right, Laney?" Will said.

"How many inches?" Laney demanded.

Will swallowed. "I'm going to lift this cloth," he said to Mia, agonizingly aware that this was wholly inappropriate and at the same time, desperately imperative.

"Just do it." Mia threw the coveralls off her and spread her knees wide. Sweat dripped down her temples in spite of the cold. "Get this frickin' baby out of me."

Okay. He put the desk lamp on the floor and angled it to shine between her legs on a view such as he'd never seen before. Her vagina gaped wide and a round dome bulged in the opening. His heart rate tripled but awe superseded fear as he witnessed the miracle unfolding. "I can see its head!"

"I've got to push," Mia yelled. Another contraction hit her and her veins stood out like cords.

"Measure!" Laney ordered.

Quickly he held the ruler in place. The opening grew bigger before his eyes. A thin bloody liquid oozed out. He swallowed, feeling his head swim. Then he straightened his spine. This was no time to be a wuss. Mia was the one experiencing all the pain and doing all the work. "Six and a half inches. No, make that seven."

"So fast, just like our mother," Laney said.

"I'm going to be sick," Mia groaned as the contraction receded and she collapsed onto the hay again.

Will handed her an empty trash can. As she gagged into it, he turned to Laney on the phone. "Can she push?"

"On the next contraction, tell her to bear down." Laney went on to explain in detail what to expect when the baby's head emerged, how to unwrap the cord from the neck and turn the shoulders.

Will kneeled on the hay, waiting with a clean towel. There must be lots Laney wasn't telling him, like what would happen if Mia did tear, or if she started bleeding profusely, or if the baby needed resuscitation. But he wasn't going to think about that. Nothing bad was going to happen and if it did, he would deal with it.

Women were tough. He'd always known that but he'd never seen it illustrated so graphically. Mia pushed on the next contraction and uttered a strangled scream. The world shrank to a space even smaller than the office, to a bed of hay and coveralls and the half-naked, sweating, grunting woman laboring to bring a baby into the world.

It all happened quickly, no more than five hard pushes and the baby's head popped out. While Mia rested and panted from her exertion, Will, with shaking hands, slipped a finger beneath the cord to lift it clear of the neck. That was the worst, right? The baby's red, wrinkled face, streaked with a white waxy substance, wasn't moving. Before Will had time to worry Mia was bearing down again and on her long, agonized groan, the baby's shoulders broke free and the baby slithered out and into his trembling outstretched hands.

Oh God. Oh God. Oh God. Laughing, exulted, Will held the baby up for Mia to see. "You did it. It's born. You have a baby boy."

The baby let out a cry, his tiny fists scrunched as tightly as his face. He was alive and letting the world know. Tears sprang to Will's eyes. If anyone had told him beforehand he would have to deliver a baby, he would have run a mile. Now that it was over he knew it would be a night he would never forget if he lived to be a hundred.

He laid the baby on Mia's stomach. The click of the digital clock made him glance over. Three minutes past midnight on Christmas morning.

Chapter Two

"HE'S SO BEAUTIFUL." Overwhelmed by a sense of wonder, Mia held her baby, laughing and crying at the same time. The pain of moments ago vanished in a blur. This wriggling, slippery creature sprawled across her stomach, his little ribs pumping like bellows, was her son.

"He's got a good pair of lungs," Will said.

Will. She felt as if she was noticing him for the first time. A lock of dark blond hair fell over his forehead and his blue eyes shone as he kneeled before her looking as proud as if this was his own baby. And he should be proud. He'd rolled up the sleeves of his blue chambray shirt and labored alongside her. She should have felt self-conscious about her exposed state and bodily fluids leaking everywhere but somehow his calm manner made it seem natural and normal. As of course it was.

"Thank you," she whispered. "I don't know what I would have done without you."

He shrugged off her thanks. "I only followed your sister's directions."

"Laney." Mia glanced at the phone. She hadn't heard a peep from her in ages. "Is she still there?"

"Hello?" Will spoke into the phone. After a pause he tried to redial then looked at Mia and shook his head. "Either her phone ran out of battery or the storm is affecting the signal."

The baby cried again. Mia pushed up her top and bra and guided his head so he could latch on. Instinctively he rooted against her breasts, his mouth opening and closing. Then he closed on the nipple, sucked a couple of times and fell asleep. Automatically Mia glanced at Will and smiled with delight. Will grinned back. It was so weird. He was a stranger. And yet, not a stranger, not anymore. They'd just been through the most intense half hour of her life.

"Lay this over him so he doesn't get cold." Will draped a clean towel across the baby. "How are you feeling? Warm enough? Do you want my coat to put over your legs?"

"Um, we have to cut the cord," Mia said. "And deliver the placenta."

"Placenta?" The poor man paled. "Right, okay. How do we do that?"

"From what I've read, you push on my stomach while I bear down. But maybe you should cut the cord first."

He opened a desk drawer and found a ball of string and a pair of scissors. "I'll sterilize these. Won't take long. I'll go boil a kettle in the kitchenette."

Before he left he spread out his sheepskin coat over her

lower half and then hurried out, shutting the door to keep the heat in.

Mia propped herself on an elbow, mesmerized by her sleeping baby. He was worn out by the birth, poor little guy. She checked his hands and feet, counting fingers and toes. She couldn't remember everything that went into an Apgar score but he was breathing freely, his color was good and he looked healthy. Her chest swelled with the immensity of her love for this tiny, fragile human being. Her baby—and Jared's.

Tears slipped from her eyes and rolled down her cheeks. She made no effort to stop them. Jared should have been here to watch his son being born, to hold him in the first minutes of his life. The joy in her heart mingled with pain, grief and anger. No matter what Jared's faults were, it wasn't fair that he couldn't be present at the birth of his child because he'd given his life in the service of his country.

"It's okay, little one, we've got each other," she murmured, aware she was comforting herself as much as the baby. "It's just you and me now."

And that's the way it was going to stay. She would get her life back together, find a place to live, another job and focus on providing her son with a stable home. Non-essentials would not distract her and that included men. No problem there. Since Jared she hadn't been interested in romance and not just because she was pregnant. Love was no guarantee of a happy marriage. One major mistake in that arena was enough to last a lifetime.

The door opened. Will held a saucepan of boiled water with the scissors and string inside. He took in her tear-stained face and then his gaze went to the bare ring finger on her left hand. His brow furrowed as if he couldn't figure out why she was doing this alone. "Do you want to call your partner? Is he…in the picture?"

Fresh tears cascaded and this time she brushed them away. Damn hormones. Mutely she shook her head, swallowing around the lump in her throat. "My husband was killed in action in Iraq—eight months ago."

"I'm so sorry." Seemingly at a loss for words, Will crouched on the floor. Her foot was the only part of her accessible so he held her ankle. His hand was warm and comforting. "Did he know about the baby?"

She shook her head, not wanting to talk about Jared, and tried to sit up. "We should do this."

"Of course." Then Will was all business, tying a knot around the cord near the baby's navel, making sure it was good and tight. "I'll bet my Scout leader never thought I'd be using a reef knot for this purpose." Sitting back on his heels he presented her with the scissors.

She tried to sit up higher but there was nothing to lean against and it was too awkward. "You do it."

Jared should have been here to cut the cord. But try as she might, she couldn't quite picture him being as adept as Will. Jared would make jokes and entertain her but could he have arranged everything on short notice and been so competent? Going on past experience… No, don't compare. It wasn't fair to Jared who'd obviously proved what he was capable of under pressure. Hadn't he saved three men in the line of fire? He had to be pretty competent to do that. All the same, she was grateful Will had been on hand tonight.

With a snip it was done.

"What are you going to call him?" Will asked.

"Jared. After his father."

Will nodded. "Good choice."

Thoughtfully, she stroked the baby's cheek with a delicate fingertip. "Is Will short for William?"

"That's right."

"Jared William…Tempesta." At the last second she substituted her maiden name for her married name. It sounded just fine. Perfect, in fact.

"Seriously? You're naming him after me? That's awesome." Grinning, Will picked up his phone. "Let me take a photo for his baby book. Otherwise no one will believe he was born in a virtual manger on Christmas Eve."

Mia arranged her clothing for modesty. "Am I decent?"

"You look like a Madonna." He snapped the photo then showed it to her.

Oh my. Her hair was a tangled mess of long dark waves and her cheeks were tracked with tears but through the strain and fatigue her eyes shone with fierce joy.

She'd lost her husband, her house and her job but she'd

gained a son—a precious, precious baby. Nothing else mattered. Everything she did from now on would be for him.

A strong cramp in her abdomen made her remember she still had work to do. "The placenta."

Will's high cheekbones seemed more pronounced in the shadows thrown by the desk lamp. "Tell me again what to do."

She told him what she remembered from her prenatal classes and the books she'd read. He placed his splayed hands over her stomach and she was surprised at how warm they were and how strong. Shutting her eyes, she bore down. It took a couple of tries but she was rewarded with a final gush as she delivered the placenta. "Ugh, sorry. Birth is such a messy business. The coveralls, your office…"

"Don't be sorry," Will said. "I wouldn't have missed this for the world."

From the tone of his voice she knew he meant it but suddenly Mia felt very tired, cold and hungry. She hadn't stopped for dinner in her hurry to get to Laney's house and now the evening's events were catching up with her. The straw no longer felt so soft and she was aware that she was sweaty and bloody, and physically and emotionally exhausted. She wished she was in a clean, warm hospital bed with a doctor checking her baby and assuring her everything was as it should be. Not that she was ungrateful. If Will hadn't been there, things would have been so much worse.

He seemed to read her mind, or maybe he could see she was drooping. "We need to get you cleaned up and to a hospital."

He brought her a bucket of warm water, a fresh towel and a wad of paper towels plus yet another pair of coveralls because her pants were soaked with snow and her waters. Then he rigged up a cherry packing box as a makeshift bassinet and lined it with another towel. He removed his shirt and took off his undershirt, giving Mia a brief glimpse of his naked, muscled torso as he wrapped the baby in the soft cotton and placed him in the nest. After putting his shirt back on Will found a wool sweater and laid it over the baby like a blanket.

Mia felt her son's forehead. It was warm and his tiny hands were warm, too. She bent her head and listened to him breathe. She hadn't noticed that Will had left the office until he returned and handed her a steaming mug and a cellophane packet. "This should tide you over till you can get something more substantial."

"Hot chocolate and a mince meat tart. Bless you! I'm starving." Gingerly she lowered herself into the office chair, wincing at the pressure on her tender bottom despite the padding of the paper towels. How had he known to bring her those when it hadn't even occurred to her that she would need them? "Are you married? Have kids?"

"No," he said shortly. "Neither."

She sipped her hot chocolate, bitter and sweet, and wondered at his abruptness. He was taking pains to adjust the lining of the cherry packing box. Starr Orchards. "Is your name Will Starr?"

"That's right."

"I've heard of your cherries. In fact, I've bought them from my local produce market in Billings," she said wonderingly. "They were delicious, so crisp and sweet. I never would have thought, when I was eating them last summer, that the man who grew them would deliver my baby. It's so cool."

"The world is full of crazy coincidences." His hands stilled on the wool sweater as he gazed at her, giving her the oddest feeling that he was touching *her*. The long night and lack of sleep must be making her hallucinate.

She cleared her throat. "Do you think the roads will be clear? Could we call an ambulance to take me to the hospital?"

"No point," he said. "I can drive you there faster."

"A taxi then," she said. "I've put you out enough already. It's Christmas morning. You'll want to be with your family."

"Sit tight and drink your chocolate. It will take me a few minutes to dig my truck out." Will grabbed his sheepskin jacket off the back of a chair and draped it around her shoulders. "I'll be right back."

He went out into the night. Mia watched him walk past the window in just his shirt, head bowed against the wind. His good nature must surely be sapped by now but he was still helping her. She ate the mince tart, savoring every flaky crumb, and watched her baby sleep. He still had traces of white vernix around his ears. Such tiny ears. He was here, at last. Over the long months alone she'd sometimes felt it would never happen. Now she'd given birth under conditions that made it seem surreal. The overheated office, the cavernous dark shed with mysterious machines, the bed of straw...

"Billy," she imagined herself saying to her son in a few years when he'd done something naughty. "Just because you were born in a barn doesn't mean you can act like an animal." She giggled and then sighed. Definitely delirious.

Billy. The name had popped up from her overtired brain but it seemed to suit him. Had she really named her child after a complete stranger? Jared had been the top of her list of names but now that her son was here, she found it didn't suit a tiny baby. Jared Junior? Jared the third? She shuddered. Absolutely not. William was too big a name and she couldn't call him Will. That would be too...intimate.

Paper towels. She couldn't get over the fact that he'd thought of them. It was embarrassing and sweet at the same time.

She looked at her watch. He'd been gone twenty minutes. She'd drunk the chocolate down to the grainy dregs and dabbed up every crumb of pastry with a forefinger. She was sore and stiff and when she moved she was aware she was still bleeding. Was that normal? Maybe she should call an ambulance. When she checked her watch next, thirty minutes had passed. He must have changed his mind, decided he'd made a mistake getting involved. Or got caught up doing something else. How many times had Jared said he would be home in half an hour and three or four hours would go by? Eventually she would find out he'd been at the casino and had lost track of time, or wanted to win his money back.

If Will wasn't here in five minutes she would call a taxi. He'd taken his phone with him but there was a landline. She opened drawers in the desk until she found a phone book. She had the page open to Taxis when headlights bumping up and down illuminated the snow banked up outside.

He'd come back. A shaft of relief and gratitude speared through her. Mia gathered up her baby out of the cherry box. He felt weightless and insubstantial in the bulky swaddling of wool and towel as she tucked him inside Will's sheepskin jacket close to her chest.

Will came in stamping the snow off his boots. "Ready to go?"

"Yes." She turned away to hide the rush of tears. "I owe you big time."

"You owe me nothing," he said. "If a person needs help, you help, that's all."

Maybe, but one day, she would find a way to repay him for his kindness and generosity.

Outside, the snow had stopped. Mia lifted her face to the

sky. A few scattered stars twinkled between the heavy shoals of slate gray clouds. An extra bright star appeared. Good omen. And then she remembered what day it was.

She turned to Will. "Merry Christmas."

He smiled at her. "Merry Christmas."

An icy blast of wind hit her face and she instinctively held her baby tighter, snug inside her jacket. Maybe equally instinctively, Will's arm went around her as he guided her to the truck. She hesitated, then allowed herself to lean on him. Tomorrow she would start being self-sufficient.

Chapter Three

SHE'D NAMED HER baby after him. Will couldn't get over it. The knowledge seemed to give him a new sense of purpose. He drove even more carefully than usual. After all, he'd brought this baby into the world and now he had to protect it. Mia and her baby seemed okay but he wouldn't feel easy until he saw them safely to the hospital.

As he slowed at the corner of Ralston Road and Finley Road, Mia pointed to a red compact sedan tilted over and half in the ditch. "That's my car."

"You walked all the way from here to the shed in a snow-storm while in labor?" he said, incredulous. "You're one tough cookie."

"I followed your Christmas lights." Her sleeping baby was tucked next to her, inside his jacket. Her dark hair billowed and tangled around her heart-shaped face. "The colors shone through the white and they were all I could see at times. They guided me to shelter, like a modern star of Bethlehem."

When he thought of how close he'd come to not putting

up the lights this year… After Katie dumped him and he'd lost the holiday spirit, stringing lights seemed a nuisance. He would never feel that way again. When the time came to put them up again he would remember Mia struggling through the snow and how they'd saved her.

"Next year I'll put up more lights," he said. "Plus maybe a reindeer and a Santa's sleigh."

"Oh, good," she said, eyes shining as if she was already looking forward to it. "I *love* Christmas decorations—the more extravagant and outrageous, the better."

Halfway to Polson they passed the spot where the tanker had gone off the road. Police had set out orange cones, diverting traffic from four lanes down to two around the jack-knifed truck lying on its side. The crumpled cab was half-buried in snow and a dirty white pickup with the passenger side bashed in sat across the oncoming lane. A couple of highway patrol cars were parked near it and officers were conferring with the driver of a tow truck. If ambulances had been required they'd already come and gone.

Mia craned her neck to look as they went slowly past. "I hope no one was injured." She shivered. "I drove this road not long before the tanker crashed. It could have been me where the white pickup was."

Will touched her hand that rested protectively on her baby's head. "Don't think of what could have happened. You're safe now."

She sat back against the seat and closed her eyes. For a

moment he thought she'd fallen asleep but then she said, very quietly, "You never know when your time will run out."

Will navigated between the cones and then pulled back onto the highway where only one lane each way had been plowed. Was she thinking of her late husband? She had to be missing him badly. He cleared his throat. "Life is hard sometimes."

"It is." She brushed her lips over baby's head. "Then something happens that makes all the bad stuff worthwhile." She paused. "Well, almost."

Will concentrated on the road. It had started snowing again: light flakes that flew into his headlights. He couldn't see far ahead and even though he knew this road like the back of his hand, the snow and the darkness made it feel unfamiliar. "Had you been married long?"

"Two years."

"Such a short time." Will could only imagine what she must be feeling. Mia's mouth turned down and he kicked himself for bringing it up. She must have really loved the guy.

"Welcome to Polson" a sign read, followed by a stretch of car dealerships, motels and fast food outlets. Will turned off to the hospital and a few minutes later parked near the main entrance.

His heart got a jolt when he looked up at the Emergency sign. The last time he'd been here was the previous July when his father had a heart attack. Thankfully his dad had survived but the whole family had been stunned to learn that a guy named Alex, who'd signed on to pick cherries, was in actual fact, Robert's son by another woman. Will had forgiven his father and welcomed Alex as his half brother but he still got a small rush of anger when he thought of when he was six years old and his dad had secretly gone back and forth between him and his mom and the other family.

He pushed the inconvenient emotions down and helped Mia inside. A huge Christmas tree stood in the center of the lobby surrounded by presents donated for sick children. Red ropes of tinsel were strung along the counter at Reception.

While Mia filled in admission forms Will held her sleeping baby. He glanced over her shoulder, noting her details. Place of residence: Billings. Occupation: cellar door manager. Age: twenty-eight.

"Anything else you want to know about me?" she murmured. "I thought seeing all my gory lady parts would have been enough information for one lifetime."

He chuckled, appreciating the fact she could joke after her traumatizing experience. "Which vineyard do you work at? I know a few wine growers near Billings."

Her fingers tightened around the pen as she filled in the last few lines. "*Worked*, emphasis on past tense. I lost my job yesterday. Boss fired me because I was having a baby." She passed over the form to the receptionist. "Nice Christmas present, huh?"

Will swore under his breath. Whoever her asshole employer was, it couldn't be anyone he knew.

A cheery middle-aged nurse in blue uniform top and pants appeared pushing a wheelchair. "I'm Anne. Come with me, hon, and I'll take you up to maternity."

Mia sank into the wheelchair and Will lowered her baby into her arms. Anne was called over to talk to the nurse at Reception, leaving them alone for a moment.

"Goodbye, Will, and thanks for everything." Mia's dark eyes, huge and tired, were filled with gratitude.

"Save the goodbyes for when the time comes." He wanted to make sure Mia got a bed. Sometimes hospitals parked people in corridors for extended periods and he didn't want that to happen to her.

Anne came back and he strode alongside as the nurse pushed the chair. In answer to Anne's questions, Mia related the tale of her son's birth on a bed of straw in a cherry packing shed. Will noticed she played down her own struggle and instead shone a light on his role.

"You did good, Dad," Anne said, giving him a smile.

Will threw Mia an apologetic glance before correcting the nurse. "I'm not the father. I just happened to be in the right place at the right time."

"Oh, I see," Anne said delicately.

"My husband passed away." Mia didn't elaborate further but Will noted the fine lines of tension tightening her face.

"Does your baby have a name yet?" Anne asked.

"Jared William," Mia replied. "I'm going to call him Billy."

Will's attention snapped at hearing his childhood nickname. "My mom called me Billy when I was little."

Her eyes widened. "No way. That is such a coincidence."

Coincidence, or something more? Maybe he was lightheaded with fatigue but it seemed to him there had to be a reason he'd been the one to be there for Mia and her baby.

"She'll get straight into a bed, won't she?" he asked Anne as they approached the nurses' station decorated in wreaths and colored baubles. A small spruce tree wound with silver garland stood in the corner opposite. "She's been through a lot tonight."

"Yes, the ward is quiet at the moment." Anne turned right along the corridor and wheeled Mia into an empty room. "I'll take this little man," she said, gently taking the baby from Mia's arms. "While I check his measurements, you can shower in there." She nodded to a washroom with the door ajar. "Put on a hospital gown and hop into bed. The doctor will be around soon to check out you and your baby." To Will, she said, "You might as well go home and get some sleep. You can come back later." She bustled out with the baby.

Mia turned to Will. "You don't need to come back. You've done so much already."

Not come back? It was unthinkable. He felt a connection to Mia and Billy now. He couldn't go home and just forget about them. He needed to know that they would be all right.

"You'll want some things from your car," he said. "Your purse, phone, toothbrush."

"Oh, right. Well, if you don't mind." She patted her pockets but she was wearing his jacket. "I must have left my keys in your office. I can't remember putting them down."

"I'll find them. Don't worry." He touched her shoulder. "Get some rest and I'll see you later."

He left the hospital feeling punch-drunk and elated. It was nearly three in the morning and he hadn't slept but he didn't feel tired, just energized. Billy was a tiny miracle that had come just when he needed one.

NEVER HAD A shower felt so good or a bed so welcome. The doctor came, inspected Mia inside and out, put in two stitches to repair a small tear, did a belated Apgar assessment on Billy, and pronounced them both fine. Anne had brought Billy to her wrapped in a soft green blanket. She'd shown Mia how to get the baby to latch on to her breast and after a few tries he'd nursed. Then he'd gone to sleep and Mia had taken a long nap.

When she woke up it was nearly two in the afternoon. Blinking at the fluorescent light and bright, hard surfaces around her, it took her a moment to realize she was in the hospital. Then yesterday's events flooded back. The night before felt like a dream compared to the prosaic surroundings of the maternity ward. The snowstorm, the car crash, the sanctuary of the warm, straw-bedded office, the almost mystical connection she'd felt with Will as she labored and gave birth—all of it felt unreal now that she was safely through it.

Which was just as well since she preferred not to remember certain aspects. She'd been so intent on seeing her sister that she'd convinced herself she could reach Sweetheart before the snowstorm hit and had jumped in the car without making sure she had plenty of phone battery. The whole episode was a reminder that acting on impulse never failed to get her in trouble. First marrying Jared and now this.

A dried-out turkey and cranberry sandwich sat on her tray. She must have slept through lunch. The curling ends of the bread reminded her of the days when she worked late and Jared had 'cooked dinner' by ordering in. Oh, he would have happily taken her out to eat at a fancy restaurant seven days a week but once she'd seen his bank balance she'd put her foot down. She wished she could take back those harsh words she'd uttered. He'd made amends, at least tried to, and now he was gone and it was too late to forgive him.

Pushing away the tray of food, she raised the head of her bed so she could look at Billy asleep in the bassinet. Fine dark hair covered his head and she could see his eyes moving beneath the near-transparent lids. Did babies this young dream, and if they did, what did they dream about—floating blissfully in the womb or the painful struggle to leave it?

"Knock, knock." Will appeared in the doorway carrying her overnight case plus an insulated bag and a third carry bag. He'd showered and shaved and changed into black denims and a forest green pullover beneath a dark gray down jacket. "How are you feeling?"

"Good." She pushed back a lock of wavy dark hair that she'd slept on wet.

He set the suitcase on the floor and started emptying the insulated bag. "What would you like first—food, presents, or your toiletry bag?"

"You didn't need to bring me anything—Oh!" The aroma of a hot turkey dinner wafted her way as he brought out a covered plate.

"I hated to think of you having Christmas all alone in the hospital so I brought some leftovers from our family lunch. I made the stuffing. It's my specialty."

"Food first, please." Her stomach rumbled as he set a plate on her bed tray. "Delicious," she said around her first bite of turkey and gravy.

"It's not Christmas without gifts, so…" He reached into another bag and came out with two wrapped presents. "They're second-hand, of course. Stores aren't open today."

"You're spoiling me." Reaching for one, she peeled back the paper to uncover three books, all well-thumbed—a mystery, a fantasy and a romance.

"I didn't know what you liked to read so I brought a selection," Will said.

"I read everything." She took in details of his appearance she'd missed last night. The wide spacing of the blue eyes, the thickness of his dark blond hair, the strong jaw and straight nose. A modern Paul Newman. Handsome in an old-fashioned way that was more about character than glossy good looks. Thoughtful as well as competent. "Thank you."

The present for Billy was flat and soft. An item of clothing? She opened it and unfolded a quilted baby blanket embroidered with cherry trees in blossom and overhead, stars in a twilight sky. 'Billy' was stitched in red across the green grass at the bottom. It was hand-sewn and worn at the edges as if it had been washed many times.

"It's beautiful," Mia said, stroking the soft fabric. "But I can't accept it."

"Yes, you can," Will said. "With the name, it's perfect."

"Did your mother make it? Does she know you're giving away your baby blanket?"

"It's mine to do what I like with."

"You should save it for your own child," she insisted.

He froze for a millisecond, his big hands twisting his beanie, then changed the subject. "I towed your car out of the ditch. You hit a stump under the snow. Twisted the tire rim and pulled the rack end out of the steering rack and bent the lower control arm."

Mia blinked. "I have no idea what you're saying but it doesn't sound good."

"It'll take a couple of days to get fixed, maybe longer

with the holidays and depending on whether the garage has parts in stock. I can tow it to Damon's Garage if you like." He pulled her phone out of his jacket pocket. "I charged this for you. Looks like your sister called. I imagine she's wondering what happened."

"Thanks for taking care of my car," Mia said. "I'll pay you back for everything, I promise."

"No rush." He waved a hand. "I added my number to your phone so if you need anything, just give me a call."

"I'll be fine now, thanks to you." She turned her phone on and sure enough, there were several messages from Laney.

Ran out of juice. What's happening?

Still stuck in Butte.

RU OK????

Quickly she texted back. *Mom and baby AOK. In hospital in Polson. Will call later.*

"Everything good with your sister?" Will asked.

"She's on her here way now," Mia lied, not wanting Will to feel responsible or put himself out for her again. "I'll see her soon."

"So she's what, hired a Sherpa to help her hike over the mountains?" Will asked with an innocent air. "Or is she part mountain goat?"

Mia pleated the blanket beneath her fingers. "I don't know what you mean."

"I heard on the news there's a big rock fall in the pass,"

he said. "It'll take days to clear."

"Busted." She gave him a sheepish grin.

"Where will you go when you leave here?" he asked. "Anne says that since you have no complications, you're going to be discharged tomorrow." When she didn't answer, he added, "I can help you find a place to stay."

"No, Will, you've done too much already. I very grateful but I don't want to impose on you." She'd never had any trouble standing on her own two feet—until Jared's gambling had cost them the house—and she was determined to get back to being self-sufficient. "I-I'll go to a hotel. No, I'll go to Laney's. She left a key hidden outside for me."

He gave her a narrow-eyed look. "Are you sure?"

She smiled brightly. "Positive."

"Well, okay." Will glanced at the bassinet. "Mind if I have a peek?"

"Go ahead," Mia said. "He's sleeping."

Will rounded the foot of the bed and peered into the bassinet. "Actually, he's not. His eyes are open and he's making guppy motions with his mouth." Will stroked Billy's cheek with the tip of a forefinger and the baby turned his head toward it. Will gave Mia a wide, warm smile. "Did you see that?"

"It means he's hungry. Can you pass him to me?"

"I've never held a baby this small before." He scooped up the swaddled babe, one hand under Billy's head and one supporting his bottom. Instead of handing Billy straight to her Will lifted him up with a goofy tender smile. "Hey, there, kid. Happy Birthday. Don't barf on your new blanket, okay? You might want to pass it on to some other deserving youngster someday."

One tiny hand broke free of the blankets, opening and closing like a starfish. Billy stared fixedly at Will as if imprinting on him—memorizing his face and the sound of his voice.

Will lowered Mia's son to her, stroking the top of Billy's head. He turned away as she opened her gown and positioned the baby to nurse. "I should go."

He sounded wistful, which was odd. He had family and no doubt friends. And even though he didn't have a wife or children of his own, a gorgeous guy like Will would have women lining up to go out with him.

"Thank you again for everything," she repeated. He was probably getting sick of her saying that but she was tired of feeling helpless and dependent. "If I don't see you again…"

"I'll pick you up tomorrow and take you to your sister's." Will held up a hand when she started to protest. "It's no big deal."

It was to her. After a year coping on her own, she could have wept, it felt so wonderful to have backup. The problem was, she didn't need the distraction of a gorgeous guy at this point in her life. And she sure as hell didn't have the emotional energy for it.

Yesterday, circumstances—the blizzard, her weak physical condition and being responsible for a newborn—had compelled her to accept his help. He'd delivered Billy and she'd named her son after him. They were inextricably linked, bonded by Fate. She couldn't deny it, no matter how much she wanted to. But she couldn't keep leaning on him.

"I'll be fine on my own," she said firmly. "You have a Merry Christmas."

Chapter Four

WILL, NATURALLY, DISREGARDED Mia's refusal of help. If anyone needed and deserved a hand, it was her. On the way to the hospital the next morning he stopped off at a friend's house to borrow a rear-facing car seat for the baby and hand-me-down newborn clothes.

"Thanks, Jen," Will said. "These things will be much appreciated."

"It's nice to see them put to use." Jen came out to the porch with her eleven-month-old baby girl in her arms. Jen's light brown hair whipped around her face in the chill breeze as she glanced up at the opaque white sky. "Looks like more snow."

"Another foot, according to the weatherman." If that was the case, Mia's sister wouldn't be getting back to town anytime soon. Will opened the back door and stowed the baby gear.

"No rush returning the car seat. In fact, keep it. This little monkey is the last, aren't you, sweetie?" Jen said, tickling under her daughter's chin and making her giggle. "Four is plenty."

Will smiled easily, but he was covering deep layers of hurt and sadness. If he and Katie were getting married as they'd planned since high school, he might have been looking forward to being a father himself in the next year or two. Then he checked himself. He had to stop thinking like that and move on.

He headed out to Route 35 and turned right to Polson. A few light flakes were already starting to fall. Half an hour later he was cruising the baby aisles of a discount drugstore. He hoped that by giving Mia second-hand and inexpensive items she would find it easier to accept them. Garret, his brother, had wondered why he was going to so much trouble for a woman he barely knew. Cody, the youngest in their family, wondered why Will hadn't been put off women completely after what Katie had done to him. But they hadn't been at the birth and they didn't know Mia. She was special in a way he couldn't define.

He arrived at the hospital on the dot of four p.m. Anne, who had become his ally, had told him that was when Mia would be discharged. No one with a newborn baby should have to take a taxi home, especially when she might not have a home to go to. He wouldn't be satisfied until Mia was safely inside her sister's house and he knew the heat was on and the lights were working.

Carrying the car seat, he took the elevator to the third floor and continued down the corridor past the nurses' station. As he approached Mia's room, he heard her talking to Anne.

"I brought my baby here in a cherry box and I'm going to carry him out that way," Mia was saying. Hands on her hips, her dark wavy hair flowing over the shoulders of a red jacket, she was nose to nose with the implacable nurse. "Would you please call a taxi?"

"Sorry, hon," Anne said, equally determined. "You're not leaving without a car seat and a taxi isn't necessary because Will is coming to get you."

"No, he won't," Mia replied. "I told him not to."

"You don't know Will Starr very well, do you?" Anne pushed the wheelchair closer. "He'll be here any minute so get in."

"I'm not getting in that chair again," Mia said. "I can stand on my own two feet."

"You can start being independent tomorrow," Will said, stepping into the room. "I've got a car seat and my truck is downstairs. I'll take you to your sister's place. Okay, Mia?"

"You came." Surprise, and what looked like relief, flashed in her eyes.

"I said I would." This was the second time she'd been surprised he'd shown up. What had she been through that she didn't trust a guy meant what he said?

"Well, since you're here." Mia went quiet. With a bit of fumbling and some help from Anne, she got Billy strapped into the car seat, his tiny knit beanie pulled down over his ears and the blanket tucked up to his chin.

"Goodbye and thanks for everything." Mia gave Anne a warm hug. "I'm still not getting in that wheelchair."

"It's the law," Will said peaceably. He just looked at her until she sighed heavily and sat. Then he picked up Billy in the car seat, handed Mia the cherry box, and grabbed Mia's bags in his other hand.

Anne, pushing the wheelchair, said to Will, "You'll have to learn to pick your fights."

Chuckling, he nodded to the nurse. "Reckon I will."

Mia's sister Laney lived on Sweet Street opposite the high school in a blue-painted bungalow with white trim. A smooth blanket of snow three feet deep covered the entire yard and driveway, right up to the front door.

"Any idea where that key might be?" Will had a snow shovel in the back but it would be good to narrow down the options.

"I'll call Laney and find out." Mia got out her phone. "Hey, Laney. I'm at your house. Where do you leave your spare key?" There was a pause. "Oh. Okay. Any news on that rock fall? Do you know when you'll be back?" She listened again, said goodbye and hung up. "She took the key in. The plant pot it was under broke."

"Do your parents live nearby?" Will asked.

"They live in Billings but they're in Italy at the moment caring for my *nonna* who broke her hip," Mia said. "I don't know anyone else in the area."

"All right then, we go to Plan B," Will said. "Ordinarily my parents would be happy to have you but they're full up over the holidays with family and visitors."

"I'll go to a motel," Mia said. "Is there one nearby?"

"The Montreau Hotel but it's pricey. There's also the Lake View Motor Inn but it's a ways out of town and there's no place nearby to shop or eat."

"Then I'll go to the Montreau."

"Let me call ahead and see if they have a vacancy." He located the number on his phone and spoke to the clerk on the desk, who told him they were fully booked until after New Year. "No go," Will said to Mia.

Billy had woken and was fretting. Mia reached between the seats to put a hand on his blanket and made a soothing sound. "He's hungry."

"Let me think." Will cranked the heater up and sat there with the engine idling. "My half brother Alex, and his wife Emma, have a house on this street and plenty of room. But they left this morning for Mexico. Alex missed out on a trip there before he met Emma and now they're going together."

"Could you take me back to Polson?" Mia said. "I'm sure I'll find a motel there."

"You could stay at my place but the house is under construction," Will went on. "The only rooms finished are my bedroom and the bathroom."

"I couldn't impose on you," Mia protested over Billy's crying. "It'll have to be Polson."

"Or, you could stay in the cottage we keep for pickers in the summer," Will suggested. "It has a kitchenette and a bathroom. It's basic but comfortable, like a budget motel. You'd have privacy and be close to town for when your sister gets back."

Mia turned to gaze out the window, her knuckles pressed to her mouth.

"Mia?" Will said.

She cleared her throat and faced him with a bright smile, eyes glittering. "You must be my guardian angel, always coming to my rescue."

"It's no big deal." He put the truck in gear and pulled away.

Angel? She might not say that if she knew the thoughts that flitted through his mind of kissing those sweet plump lips. He needed to keep those thoughts strictly to himself. She was mourning her late husband. What she needed right now was a friend. Will could be that guy—*if* he kept things platonic. It wasn't like he wasn't getting something out of this oddball partnership. Taking care of her and Billy took his mind off the gaping hole in his own life.

"OH, IT'S SO cute!" Mia exclaimed as Will ushered her into a tiny log cabin.

When Will had driven past a row of concrete block units

she'd steeled herself for linoleum floors, a camp bed, and hard chairs around a scarred table. Instead she found warm wood, soft area rugs and chintz fabric on an overstuffed couch and chair.

It was a cottage out of a fairy tale. Everything was in miniature proportions but so perfectly designed and laid out as to be both comfortable and utilitarian. She wandered through the cabin with growing delight—two bedrooms, one with a double bed and another with bunk beds, a serviceable kitchen stocked with basic pantry items, and a sparkling clean bathroom complete with guest towels and toiletries.

"My grandfather built it sixty years ago when he came to homestead in Sweetheart. He and my grandmother lived here when they were first married. The kitchen and bathroom have been renovated but a lot of it is original. You can still see Grandpa Nate's ax marks on the logs."

"And no one lives here?"

"I did for two months in the fall while my house was being framed." Will flipped on the electric baseboard heater in the living room and went into the bedroom to do the same in there. He returned to the main room, stripping off his jacket. "If you find any spare socks kicking around they'll be mine."

Knowing Will had stayed here made the cabin feel even cozier, as if his presence permeated every nook and cranny. Mia picked Billy out of the car seat and took refuge in the armchair to nurse. The heater ticked busily and soon the room was warm and toasty. After a while Billy fell asleep and she laid him back down in the car seat.

Accepting Will's help wasn't the problem, she decided. After all, she would do the same for a person in need. The problem was that at every turn, she was reminded that Jared should have been taking care of her, not a stranger. She longed to cocoon with her baby, be cosseted and cared for by Billy's daddy. To see Jared make good on his promise to turn over a new leaf and stop gambling, to pay his debts and buy a new house. He'd promised. She'd believed. Then he'd shipped out to Iraq and she'd never seen him again.

"I'll make you a hot drink," Will said, unpacking the few groceries they'd picked up on the way over from Laney's. "Coffee, tea, or Ovaltine?"

"Ovaltine, please." She'd never had the malty drink until staying in the hospital but now she craved it.

She watched him pour the milk and put the mug into the microwave. Maybe her discomfort came from knowing that Will was taking better care of her than Jared would have. Her late husband bought her champagne and jewelry but he'd never made her a hot drink. It was easier to flash the credit card than put himself out.

Will handed her the steaming mug, smiling as he met her gaze. Warmth spread through her as she murmured her thanks. She wasn't shy but something about him made her duck her head. What was wrong with her? Sure he was attractive but as a new mom, the last thing on her mind was romance.

She closed her eyes and leaned back against the chair, reaching into her mind for memories of Jared. She pushed back images of the fights and bitterness and pictured him holding her close, sharing the miracle of their baby. Clinging to thoughts of their last weekend together when Billy had been conceived, and lulled by the warmth and comfort, she drifted in and out of a light sleep.

The front door closed quietly, waking her. Her eyes opened on the unfamiliar room, the snow piled up against the window. Outside, Will's truck started up and drove away. A panicky flutter filled her chest, like the panic she'd felt six months ago when the bank foreclosed on her house and she'd had to sleep in her car for a week while she looked for a rental apartment. She could have stayed with her parents, or even her in-laws, but she hadn't wanted to admit Jared had left her in such bad straits. Last week after losing her job she'd given notice on her apartment.

Now she didn't even have a car.

She took a breath and got a grip. Will wouldn't abandon her. He would come back when he was ready, or able. No doubt he had things to do. The man had a life. He couldn't babysit her nor did she want him to.

She checked on Billy, sound asleep in his car seat. Was it good for his back to be curled like that? She rose carefully, wincing a little, and transferred him gently to the cherry box where it rested on an old chest. Billy's rosebud mouth sucked

JOAN KILBY

at air and his tiny fingers grasped but once he was laid down, he settled back to sleep. She adjusted his knitted cap and tucked Will's blanket up to his chin.

Moving slowly, she carried her cup to the sink and washed it and Will's coffee cup. Checking the cupboards she found canned soup and an unopened box of crackers. She wouldn't starve at any rate. Turning to tidy the counter she discovered Will's note. *Back later.* Relief settled over her along with an unfamiliar feeling of security and trust. And right on its heels the reminder: *don't get used to it.*

She couldn't put off calling Nora and Jed, her mother-in-law and father-in-law, any longer. Although why it felt like a chore, she didn't know. Maybe because Nora talked about Jared too much, her voice heavy with grief. Mia couldn't blame her but it weighed her down. Nora would be happy about the baby though.

"Merry Christmas, Jed," she said brightly to cover her mild dismay at getting her gruff father-in-law. If Nora was overly talkative, Jed was hard work. "I got Nora's Christmas greetings via voice message but couldn't call you back until now. I had the baby. It came early."

Jed called to his wife. "Nora, she had the baby."

Nora spoke in the background. "Put her on speaker. Hi, Mia," she said, coming into the conversation. "When did you give birth? What is it? Is everything okay?"

"Everything's fine. He's a little boy." Mia smiled, thinking back to the moment she first held her son. "Eight pounds three ounces. Born Christmas morning just after midnight. He's beautiful, absolutely perfect."

"Oh," Nora sighed. "I can't wait to see him and hold him. What's his name?"

"Jared William." Mia's hand tightened on her phone for no reason except intuition that Nora wouldn't approve her next statement. "I'm calling him Billy." Silence. "It suits him. You'll see."

"William," Jed repeated. "Is that a name from your family? It doesn't sound Italian."

"I named him after the man who delivered him." Mia related the story of the blizzard and the birth in the cherry packing shed, trying to make it sound less scary than it had been at the time.

"Oh, my goodness," Nora said. "You should never have left Billings. Didn't I say that, Jed? She should have stayed put until after the baby was born. Tempting Fate, I said, didn't I, Jed? And I was right."

"When are you coming for a visit?" Jed asked. "We have Jared's old room ready for you and Nora's fixed up the nursery for Jared Junior."

"Billy," Mia corrected him. "My car was damaged when I went off the road. It's getting fixed. I still haven't seen Laney because she's stuck in Butte. I'll come after New Year, assuming the roads are clear."

"We'll get you a new car, an SUV," Jed said. "It's time you got rid of that junker anyway. I don't know why Jared let you keep driving it."

Jared had let her keep driving it because even though he had a high-paying job and she was working, his gambling expenses meant she couldn't afford a new one. But his parents wouldn't want to hear that.

"It's fine," Mia protested. Her second-hand Honda wasn't fancy but it gave her few problems and she'd learned to change the oil and check the brakes herself.

"It broke down," Jed said. "I've got a buddy in Polson who runs a Mercedes-Benz dealership there. I'll give him a call."

"Thank you but please don't," Mia said. "My car will be fine once it's repaired."

"You don't have baby Jared sleeping on his stomach, do you?" Nora cut in. "It's not good for a newborn. What kind of a cot are you using? Are the slats close together? You don't want him getting his head caught."

"He's on his back. And he doesn't move except for waving his hands," Mia said patiently. She smiled wryly, wondering what Nora would say if she knew her grandson was sleeping in a Styrofoam box. "How are you both? Did you have a nice Christmas?"

"We missed Jared, of course." Nora's voice turned sad and held a faint note of reproach, as if they couldn't possibly have a good Christmas when their son was dead and how could Mia even suggest such a thing? "We said prayers for him and held a candlelight vigil on Christmas Eve."

"I miss him, too." She glanced at her sleeping baby's sweet, round face. "I think Billy's got his nose."

"Too soon to say," Jed declared, always ready to argue any point. "What color is his hair?"

"Dark like mine," Mia replied. "I'll send a photo. It's all been a bit crazy and I must have baby brain I'm so scattered. I should have thought of it earlier."

"Who did you say delivered your baby?" Nora asked. "I'm looking up OBGYNs at Polson General on my iPad and I don't see any with a first name William."

Nora had a tendency not to listen carefully, or maybe she heard what she wanted to hear. On the other hand, maybe Mia hadn't been clear. As well as scattered, she was tired and weak and didn't feel like doing anything except sleep. "He's not a doctor. He owns the shed where I gave birth."

"A shed. What does he do?" Jed demanded.

Mia pressed her fingers against her forehead, which had begun to ache. "He works in the family cherry orchard. Starr Orchards. I've heard of them, eaten their cherries."

"So he works with his hands." Jed spoke in the slightly disparaging tone he reserved for working-class folk.

"I hope he washed them," Nora said indignantly.

Mia thought about Will's hands when he'd delivered her baby. Strong but gentle, lightly callused, moving without fuss, economical, competent. Caring.

There was a knock at the door.

"Excuse me, someone's here," Mia said, relieved at the

interruption. "I have to go. I'll see you next week."

"You'll stay here," Jed said. It wasn't a question.

"Thank you, I will. Just until I find a new job and get back on my feet."

"There's no rush for that," Nora said. "You can stay home with the baby as long as you want."

"That's very kind but hopefully I won't have to impose on you for long. Bye now." Mia hung up. They meant well and part of her would love to be a stay-at-home mom for a while but at Nora and Jed's house that would come at too big a price. They would want to have a say in everything to do with her baby.

She levered herself to her feet then shuffled across to the door. Opening it brought an icy blast and the fresh scent of snow. A woman in her fifties with a smooth blonde bob and her face muffled by a pale blue scarf stood on the doorstep holding a covered casserole dish. Behind her was a gray-haired man carrying a paper bag. Both looked fit and outdoorsy.

"You must be Mia," the woman said warmly. "I'm Linda and this is Robert. We're Will's parents. If this isn't a good time we'll just drop these things off and go."

"It's fine. Come in." Mia stepped back and let them in. "Will isn't here. He said he'd be back later but didn't say when."

"Oh, we didn't come to see him," Linda said. "We want-ed to welcome you. I made a turkey casserole and I brought some of my homemade cherry jam. Robert, have you got the bag?" She put down her casserole dish and Robert handed over a jar of ruby red jam. "I bought this Teddy bear for my stepdaughter-in-law but she's only three months pregnant so I have plenty of time to get her another."

"Thank you so much." Mia stroked the soft brown fur, a little overwhelmed. No wonder Will was so thoughtful. He'd been raised right. "Would you like some coffee or tea?"

"No, but thank you." Linda pulled off her tan wool jacket and brown leather gloves and laid them on a kitchen chair. "Could we have a peek at your baby? I won't wake him, I promise."

"You have to forgive my wife," Robert said. "She's dying to be a grandmother."

"He's gorgeous," Linda whispered, bending over the baby. "I love that his bed is a cherry box. Did you see that, Robert? Would you mind if I took a photo for our family album? So cute with Will's baby blanket."

"I told him he should keep it for his own child someday," Mia said uncomfortably. "I plan to give it back."

"No, no, don't do that. I can always make another when…if…" Linda trailed away. "He wanted your son to have it. I think it makes him feel better about…"

"About what?" Mia inquired delicately.

Linda exchanged a glance with Robert and changed direction. "He's perked up so much since you and your baby arrived on his doorstep. You've given him quite a lift."

"Something to keep his mind busy," Robert agreed. "Winter: there's too much time to brood. He's better now that he's got something to do."

So she was a project for Will. Something to keep his mind busy. What did he need to forget? Why did that make her feel a tiny bit let down? As if she wasn't enough in herself to warrant his kindness and attention. That was crazy, her hormones talking. Wasn't it? She was so tired and confused.

She passed the Teddy bear back to Linda. "Do you want to put it in Billy's bed?"

"May I? I'd love to." Linda placed the soft toy in the corner of the box and quickly snapped a photo on her phone. "I'll send you a copy."

"I'm going to shovel the path while you girls chat," Robert announced and went back outside.

"Oh, he doesn't have to do that." Mia half rose from her chair.

"He's like Will, has to keep busy." Linda sat on the couch. "You tell me if you're tired and I'll get out of your way."

"I'm fine, thanks." Mia was surprised to find it was true. Linda was attentive but not intrusive, a reassuring presence. She gave off positive energy, not drained it.

"Are your parents close by?" Linda asked.

"They're in Italy, visiting my grandmother," Mia said. "I sent them an email with a photo and spoke briefly to my mom."

"I bet she's thrilled," Linda said. "When are they coming back?"

"I'm not sure. They planned to be back before Christmas but *Nonna* had a fall and broke her hip. They're staying longer to take care of her."

There was a knock on the door.

"I'll get it." Linda jumped up and opened to two men in their late twenties. Judging by the family resemblance these were Will's brothers. And judging by the way they swayed on their feet, they'd been imbibing some holiday spirit. "Garret, Cody, what are you doing here? I thought you were at the Wilsons' open house."

"We were, then we decided to pay our respects to the Christmas baby and mom." Garret's chestnut brown hair was cut stylishly short on the sides and full on top. His button-down shirt and skinny pants wouldn't have been out of place in a trendy restaurant in the city. Over the shirt he wore a novelty Christmas pullover with cartoon reindeer. He made an expansive gesture to Mia. "Congratulations, felicitations and our hearty thanks for choosing our shed out of all the barns and garages in Sweetheart to give birth in."

"We come bearing gifts," Cody added, producing from the various bags a bottle of champagne, a jug of eggnog, cheese and crackers, nuts and chocolates. His style was more country with his faded jeans and cowboy boots. Over his plaid shirt he wore a Santa and Mrs. Claus sweater pushed up to reveal tattooed forearms. His black hair was slicked back from his forehead and he wore a sprig of holly above his left ear.

Mia smiled at their silliness. "Thank you."

Garret presented Mia with a parcel in Christmas wrap. "To celebrate the festive occasion and your newborn. Every time you call him 'sweetheart' you'll be reminded of our wonderful town."

"Oh, you two!" Linda chided with maternal indulgence then turned to Mia. "Give them a moment to see the baby and then we'll leave you in peace, I promise."

Mia was tired but she needed her spirits lifted more than she needed to rest. The boisterous Starr clan was perfect to throw off the funk she'd been in during the past long, cold months. "No, please stay. I can't drink because I'm nursing but I might have one sip to toast. Thank you everyone for all this bounty. I…" A lump came suddenly to her throat that she, a complete stranger, had been so warmly welcomed. "Thank you."

In his cherry box, Billy cried and everyone hushed, all heads turning to the baby. Garret carefully scooped him from his nest and passed him to Cody who passed him to Linda who placed him in Mia's arms. She settled Billy to nurse.

Garret, Cody and Linda brought glasses and dishes of food and put the spread on the coffee table. Robert came in from outside, stamping his snowy feet. Before Mia knew what was happening there was a party going on. After she finished feeding Billy Linda begged to be allowed to change his diaper and carried him off to the bedroom as if he was delicate china.

Garret popped the champagne and they were just about to toast when another knock came and everyone yelled, "Come in!" because it had to be Will.

Chapter Five

"ARE WE HAVING a party?" Will took in his tipsy family, the bottles and the array of snacks. So much for trying to give Mia a place of sanctuary where she could rest up after her birth. However, although she was pale, with lines of fatigue around her eyes, she had bright spots of color in her cheeks and she was laughing at the shouted welcome. Billy, in the crook of her arm, looked alert and content. "What are we toasting? And where's my glass?"

"Here," Cody handed him a flute of bubbly. "We're drinking to your namesake."

Garret raised his glass. "To Jared William! And to Mia!"

Will tipped his glass in Mia's direction and drank. She sipped at the thimbleful of champagne in her flute, her eyes smiling at him over the rim of her glass. Her gaze wasn't provocative or sexy but he had to glance away. Something about the playfulness in her sparkling eyes, a mischievous humor in her wry smile, made his pulse stir. Not that he was going to start anything with her. She'd just given birth. More importantly, she'd lost a much-loved husband and was still in mourning. Talk about a double whammy.

While his brothers argued about which of them had the best worst Christmas sweater, Will unloaded the bag of takeout Chinese he'd bought on the counter. He hadn't planned to take part in the annual sweater contest but he'd been in such a good mood this morning that while he was in town seeing how Mia's car was coming along, he'd dropped into the local thrift shop.

"Ahem!" He took off his jacket, revealing a lurid Christmas scene incongruously depicting golden sand, palm trees and a multi-species tableau. "I think you'll all have to agree that I win."

Linda put her hands over her eyes in mock horror. "Please, make it go away."

Garret tilted his head to one side. "Is that a surfing kangaroo?"

"Christmas Down Under," Will confirmed, ridiculously gratified to have made Mia laugh. "Santa does Australia."

"It's hideous," Mia said. "Take it off."

"Ooh," Cody exclaimed, waggling his eyebrows. "When was the last time a woman said that to you, Will?"

"Stow it," Will said good-naturedly. He pulled up a kitchen chair between the couch and Mia's armchair. "You okay?" he asked her. "My family can be full on sometimes."

"Don't apologize," Mia said. "They're wonderful."

Robert leaned forward. "Will tells us your late husband served in Iraq. I'm sorry to hear of his passing. I'm sure he would have been proud of his young son."

"Yes, he would." Mia's smile faded and she fussed with Billy's blanket.

Linda, Garret and Cody were talking and laughing and hadn't noticed. But Will did and he frowned at the somber note introduced into their pleasant afternoon. Mia kept her grief to herself but he'd sensed moments when she seemed overwhelmed with loss. It was a shame that she'd been reminded just when she was relaxing and enjoying herself.

"It's getting late," Will said. "We should go and let Mia rest."

"It's all right," she said to him, then turned to Robert. "Thank you for saying that. Jared would have been proud. He wanted to have children, especially a son."

"What happened to him?" Robert asked. "If you don't mind me asking."

"Dad, is this really a fit topic for a celebration?" Will said.

"I only mean to honor the man," Robert said.

"It helps to talk about it," Mia said. "To remind myself that his death had meaning." Now the others were listening, too. "He and three other men were in Mosul, going from house to house looking for insurgents when snipers started firing at them from rooftops. Two of the men in his troop were hit. He carried one man to safety and then went back for the other man who was wounded in the leg. They were almost back to their unit when a sniper shot Jared in the neck." Her chin trembled. "H-he died instantly; that's the only consolation."

Murmurs of sympathy and comfort arose from those gathered. Robert sadly shook his head and Linda patted Mia's hand. "My dear, I'm so sorry."

Mia dabbed at her eyes. "Jared was awarded a medal of honor posthumously."

A war hero. It didn't surprise Will that she would have attracted a man of sterling character. Seeing the naked emotion on Mia's face for her late husband nearly nine months after his death, it was clear she was still deeply in love with him.

"We should sing carols," Linda announced. "Will left early on Christmas Eve and we didn't get to them. I think it would be appropriate now."

Will and his brothers groaned but the token protest was another ritual of the Starr Christmas. They all enjoyed carol singing, even Will, who couldn't carry a tune in the proverbial bucket.

"Really?" Mia brightened. "I love carols. But we don't have any music or lyrics."

"I came prepared," Linda said, bringing a sheaf of songbooks out of her handbag.

"My guitar might still be in the closet from when I was staying here." Will went to look and sure enough, his scarred but serviceable acoustic guitar was lying on the top shelf. He carried it with him, tuning it as he walked.

Mia opened one of the songbooks on the arm of her chair and glanced up at him. "We can share."

He smiled down at her, strumming a couple of chords to begin. Mia deserved a medal herself. Not many women could crash their car in a blizzard and give birth in a shed without a doctor and be game to party with a family of strangers two days later.

He glanced around at his parents and brothers and as one they launched into "We Three Kings." Garret and Cody knew their roles, each taking a kingly solo in turn. Will's solo was the third king and he sang the measured lyrics solemnly and off key. Mia smiled at him all the way through. Funny how things turned out. Two days ago he'd been sunk in gloom. Today he felt happy for the first time in a long time.

They went on to sing every song in the book. And when Mia sang "Away In A Manger" in a sweet, clear soprano, Will had to swallow hard. His mom unabashedly blinked away tears as they all smiled at the baby in Mia's arms.

Afterward they ate Linda's casserole and the Chinese takeout. Linda and Garret cleaned up the kitchen while Robert and Cody carried out the rubbish. Will put the furniture back in place while Mia nursed Billy and changed him, ready for bed.

Mia was yawning too by the time they left at eight p.m. She walked them to the door. "Do you have far to go?"

"Our house is half a mile up the road." Linda kissed Mia on the cheek. "Thanks for putting up with us. It was lovely to meet you. Come and visit if you feel up to it."

Robert, Garret and Cody said their goodbyes. Will was the last to leave, lingering as his parents and brothers started moving to their cars.

"Sleep well," he said. "Call me if you need anything."

"Your family is so nice." She leaned against the doorway. "That was an unexpectedly good Christmas. Best I've had since I was in Italy with my uncle and his family."

"When were you there?" He should let her go to bed but it was hard to leave.

She yawned hugely, covering her mouth. "It's a long story. Another time."

"Rain check, then." Would there be another time? He'd heard on the news that the road to Butte was expected to be cleared by morning. He kissed her lightly on the temple. A platonic kiss for a new mother and bereaved widow.

Mia stepped back, gave him a last smile and closed the door.

Linda was de-icing the windows as Will walked past on the way to his truck which was parked behind his parents' Suburban. His dad was in the truck, warming up the engine. "She's lovely, Will."

"I'm glad I could help her," he said. "She's had a tough time."

His mother ran a gloved finger across the de-icer, removing the layer of frost. "Be careful, son."

His fingers curled around the keys in his pocket. "What

do you mean?"

"I mean, you're in a vulnerable state after Katie, on the rebound. I can see you like Mia—"

"Mom, come on, she's not in a position to…" He trailed off. It seemed wrong to even say the words aloud. "It's not like that."

"Okay, good, as long as you realize it can take years for people to get over the loss of a beloved partner. Sometimes they never do."

"I'm not vulnerable, not in that way," he said. "I'm trying to be a friend to her, that's all."

"I know and you're doing a great job." His mother hugged him. "How's the house going?"

"Oh, you know, coming along." He hadn't done a thing toward completing it since Katie had turned down his proposal. But enough of the third degree. "Goodnight, Mom. Thanks for everything you did for Mia."

He waved to his dad and watched them drive away. Then he got in his truck but didn't turn it on. The past couple of days had been a roller coaster of emotion and activity. Mia's arrival had shaken up his Christmas. There'd been unbelievable highs, like the moment of birth, along with anxiety that it would go well, and quietly happy times visiting Mia and Billy in the hospital. He hadn't had time to brood over Katie or kick himself for wasting years of his life in a relationship that he should have been able to see wasn't going anywhere.

A light still burned inside. Was the baby fussing? It must be hard being a single mom with no one to trade off with when you were tired. He thought about knocking and seeing if Mia needed help but then decided it might be intrusive. Maybe she was just lying in bed enjoying a peaceful moment with her baby.

He gazed up at the stars through the trees. Their crystalline twinkle against the black helped bring some vague thoughts into focus. His own mom had been a single mother for the first six years of his life and he'd often thought how hard it must have been for her emotionally in those days. It had been hard for him, too, not having a father around. Maybe part of the reason he felt such a connection to Mia and Billy stemmed from empathy. He could easily put himself in her son's place and imagine how tough life might be for the boy in the coming years.

But his mother's warning was unnecessary. Mia would be gone soon. The roads would open, she would go to her sister's house, and after that she would return to Billings and be out of his life.

Finally the lights in the cottage went out. He started the engine and drove away.

BILLY'S CRY WOKE Mia before dawn, setting off a tingling in her full breasts. She'd kept him beside her in bed during the night, afraid he would get cold sleeping by himself. Plus that way, it was easier to cuddle him and nurse. She stroked the fine dark hair on his head as he suckled. "You're doing just fine, little one. *We're* doing fine."

She loved how he closed his eyes in concentration and rested his tiny hand on her breast while he suckled as if anchoring himself to her. And when he broke away suddenly to look up into her eyes, her heart flooded with love and happiness.

She moved him to her other breast and got herself comfortable on her side, her arm curled protectively around him. He nursed for a few minutes, rested, then suckled again.

Mia dozed, her mind going over yesterday's events. It had been fun having Will's family around. It made her feel as if she hadn't missed Christmas after all. She'd seen his truck parked outside after everyone left and it was comforting how he'd waited until she'd turned out the light before leaving, as if he somehow knew she would be nervous in the strange cottage in the middle of the orchard. He made her feel safe.

That was fine for now and she couldn't be more grateful but she couldn't let him continue to do things for her. She'd noticed Linda observing Will interacting with her, and Linda's motherly concern. Was she afraid Mia would take advantage of Will's good nature? And what was that look that passed between Linda and Robert about earlier when they were talking about Will? What had happened to make them worried for their son?

The last thing Mia wanted to do was harm such a good, kind man in any way. She smiled, amused at herself. In her post-baby condition she was hardly a threat to Will's peace of mind although after months of waddling around like a blimp it did her ego good to think that a man might be attracted to her—even if Linda thought it a bad idea. Then again, mothers worried about their offspring even when there was no cause.

She drifted off. When she woke again the room was light and the clock beside the bed read 9.15. Billy was still asleep so she tucked the covers around him and got up. The rag rug next to the bed was warm but her toes curled when they hit the cold floorboards. Pulling on a dressing gown she went to the living room, turned up the heater then found a clean pair of elastic-waisted pants and a loose top—yeah, she was a femme fatale all right—and headed to the bathroom to shower.

When she got out, her phone was ringing. Dripping, she picked it off the bed and answered. "Laney, where are you?"

"I'm on my way to Sweetheart," her sister said. "The road is open. I should be there in an hour or so. How are you? How's Billy?"

"Billy is a perfect angel," Mia said. "As for me, I'm still wearing maternity clothes. How is that fair?"

"First World problems…"

"I know. I'll go count my blessings." And she had plenty to count—she was in no doubt about that. A beautiful baby, a wonderful sister, loving parents… And Will, an unexpected bonus who'd fallen into her life just when she'd most needed a boost to her spirits.

"Gotta go, the traffic light's about to change," Laney said. "Where should I pick you up?"

"I'm in a cottage in the Starr cherry orchards. Honestly, I have no idea how to get here." She walked over to the window and looked out. "It's down a lane off Ralston Road. I can see the cherry packing shed from here and a row of concrete block accommodation units. All surrounded by about a million cherry trees."

"I'll find you," Laney said.

"See you soon." Mia hung up and went back to the bedroom to check on Billy. Still asleep.

She made herself toast and ate it with Linda's cherry jam along with another cup of hot Ovaltine. Her phone rang and seeing caller ID gave her a buzz of pleasure. "Hi, Will."

"Morning," he said. "I'm heading into town. Do you need anything?"

"No, thanks to you and your family I could survive being snowed in for a month." She wandered over to the window in case he was driving past the cottage but the snowy track stretched emptily between the winter-bare trees.

"I dug out some board games and cards to pass the time," Will said. "If you like, I'll stop by later."

"My sister will be back today. I'll be out of your hair."

Silence. After a beat, he said, "That's great. Do you need

me to take you over there?"

"She'll pick me up." Had that been disappointment in his voice? She felt a bit that way, too, as if their time together had ended too early. Which was crazy since three days ago she hadn't known he existed. "What should I do with the key?

"Just leave it on the counter."

"I can't begin to thank you—" she began.

"It seems wrong to say goodbye—" he said at the same time.

"I'll be here till New Year's Day," Mia said. "We could grab a coffee." She walked back into the bedroom to check on Billy.

"I wish you were coming with me today," he blurted as if making a confession.

"Why, what's happening?" She bent low to listen and make sure Billy was breathing. At first she heard nothing and her heart almost stopped. Then came the faint sigh of his breath. Thank God.

"I'm seeing my ex to exchange personal items we left at each other's houses," Will said and Mia could picture the wry twist to his mouth. "I'd just as soon she chucked out my old CDs but she wants her stuff so I guess I'm doing this."

"Your ex." So that explained his parents' concern. "How long ago did you break up?"

"Thanksgiving. It came out of the blue," Will went on. "It's been kind of tough, the first Christmas on my own.

Nothing compared to what you've gone through of course."

If he only knew. Grief was but half her problem. "You're a great guy. Whoever she is, she must be sad to lose you."

"Not so much," Will said. "She's already engaged to another guy."

"Oh, sorry. That sucks." Mia rested a hand on Billy's chest, feeling his reassuring warmth through the blanket. "Laney won't be here for a while. I'll come with you."

"Are you sure you're up to it?" Will asked.

Not really. But she was upset on Will's behalf at that woman dumping him. And she wanted to see him. As simple and as complex as that. She wanted to feel the warmth of his hand on her arm as he helped her on the icy walk, to see him looking at her with curiosity and affection, as though they were real friends, not just ships passing in the night.

"I'll even pretend to be your new girlfriend," Mia joked. "Let her wonder whose baby I'm toting."

Will chuckled. "Nah, she knows me too well. Knows I'm not the type to lie or cheat."

Lucky Katie. Jared had never cheated on her but he'd lied plenty. "Did she cheat on you?"

"Well, now, that's a matter for debate. We've been on-again, off-again since high school but I'd thought we would end up together. We planned to marry someday. Then, wham, she blindsided me by falling in love with someone else."

Mia could hear the bitter frustration in his voice.

"Sounds like a lack of communication."

"When you know someone for that long you tend to believe that some things go without saying. But the situation changed, so yeah, she probably should have told me sooner."

"I'm coming with you," Mia said. "You don't want her to think you're pining."

"No, I do not," Will said. "I'll pick you up in half an hour. If you like, I can drop you off at your sister's place afterward."

"That would be great," she said. "I'll pack my stuff."

Mia texted Laney with the change of plans, then went into action, swapping the loose top for a more fitted one with a scoop neck that showed a hint of cleavage. She found a hairdryer in the bathroom and styled her hair. Then she put on makeup for the first time in nearly a week, making her eyelashes full and black and giving her mouth a rosy bloom.

Her bag was packed and Billy was washed and changed and placed in his car seat when Will drove up to the cottage. Mia put on knee-high boots over her pants and grabbed her down jacket, before opening the door.

Will's breath frosted the cold air. His blond hair and blue eyes dazzled against the blue sky. His long legs were encased in snug faded jeans and his sheepskin jacket was open over a thick maroon sweater. She remembered how warm the jacket had been, how sweet Billy looked tucked inside. And thought how cold Will must have been that night wearing only his shirt. How could his girlfriend have let him go? The man was clearly a keeper.

"Thanks for doing this," he said, picking up the car seat in one hand and her suitcase in the other.

"I owe you." Mia pulled on a cherry red beret over her loose, waving hair.

"No, you don't." He looked at her, head tilted.

"Okay, I don't, I just want to come," she said to avoid an unnecessary argument. But her gloved hands curled into fists. No one messed with her knight in shining armor.

Chapter Six

WILL PULLED ONTO Finley Road, heading for Sweetheart, the vast white expanse of Flathead Lake on the right. This was his first meeting with Katie since she'd told him she was engaged to Whatshisname and he dreaded it. He was still angry and hurt and wondering what the hell he'd done wrong. Katie hadn't given him any concrete reasons as to why she'd fallen out of love with him other than 'they'd been together too long.' Wasn't that what marriage was—being together for a long time?

Mia gazed out the window, her chin cupped in her palm. What was going through her head? Will checked Billy in the rearview mirror. Installing a proper anchoring bolt to hold the car seat in place was worthwhile even if Mia wasn't going to be around. He had to keep reminding himself of that fact. He'd focused on her and Billy to the exclusion of all else for days. It was hard to believe that in less than a week she would be out of his life completely.

"Tell me about Katie," Mia said, turning to him.

"We met in high school—"

"Wait, don't tell me." Mia held up a hand mischievously. "You were captain of the basketball team; she was head cheerleader. Am I right?"

"Wrong, smarty-pants." He grinned. "I was on the debating team and she edited the school newspaper."

"Oh, so you're the smarty-pants," Mia said. "I would have thought with your height and build you'd be a jock."

"I did play basketball, you were right there. Nowadays I coach. I'm only six three, not that tall these days. Although to *short* people…" he gave her a pointed look "…I must seem like a giant."

She puffed up like a bantam rooster. "Who are you calling short?"

"If the shoe fits…" he teased. "Anyway, Katie and I hooked up during our senior year. We broke up when she went away to college to study radiography. Afterward, she got a job in Kalispell and we got back together. Only to split again when she took a couple of years off to travel and then work in Houston."

"Did you date other girls when she was away?"

"Sure. She dated, too. We were always open about that sort of thing. Our separations were amicable."

"You never wanted to go with her?" Mia asked.

"I belong here." Did that made him sound like part of the landscape, like the Hendersons' barn they were passing on the left? "I've traveled some, to South America and Australia, but I like home best. I'm taking over the orchard business as my father edges toward retirement. He spends more time at his realty office these days anyway."

"Sounds as if the orchard is really important to you," Mia said.

"My grandfather, Nate Starr, planted it after the Second World War," Will said. "Dad's added to it and I have my own ideas to expand our market. I can't implement them if I'm moving around."

Mia drew lines in the condensation on her window. "Jared was in his family business, too, managing his father's hotel."

"I thought he was in the army," Will said.

"He took a break from the hotel business to serve," Mia said. "The army was…a family tradition. He only joined up six months before he was killed."

Will turned onto 3rd Avenue, heading south to Main Street and the Cherry Pit diner. The tinsel and giant candy canes attached to the lamp posts glittered in the winter sunshine. He got a small pang when he thought of all the years he'd met Katie at the Cherry Pit—for Coke floats and burgers in high school and in later years, lattes and cronuts. Seeing a parking space he pulled into a diagonal slot. He cut the engine and glanced at his watch. They were early.

"Katie and I had an unspoken agreement that one day we would marry," he said. "Everyone expected it, not only us but also our parents, our friends…" Will struggled to keep his voice steady, but even he could hear the hurt. "Last year she'd was living and working in Marietta but was planning to come home at Christmas. It seemed to me like a good time for us to make a commitment. I started building a house for us to live in. I was going to propose at Thanksgiving." He fell silent. He could hardly bear to think of that now.

"And?" Mia prompted gently.

"I took her out for dinner, did the whole romantic thing, down on one knee and produced a ring. She tried to stop me but I was on a roll and just kept going. I asked her to marry me." The remembered humiliation rushed back to fill his cheeks with heat. "That's when she told me she'd met another guy and fallen in love."

"Oh, Will." Mia stroked his hand with soothing fingertips. "How awful. It must be hard to let go. You believed you were going to spend your life with her."

"It's no big deal." He only felt like the earth had been ripped out from under his feet. "The worst part was, she'd been sleeping with this guy for seven months. We always told each other when we were seeing someone else. This time she didn't."

Mia was quiet a moment, her hand still resting on his. "It sounds to me," she said thoughtfully. "As if you two weren't as solid as you thought. Ten years is a long time to be 'sort of engaged.'"

"How long did you know Jared before you got married?"

"Only a few months." Mia smiled wistfully. "I met him while I was in Hawaii on vacation. He swept me off my feet.

He was like no one I'd ever met: exciting and romantic. Every day we did something amazing—sunset cruises, diving with sea turtles, dining and dancing under the stars. He bought me jewelry, sent flowers daily, was so attentive I didn't stand a chance."

Was that what true love looked like? If so, Will was screwed. He only knew how to show his caring in practical ways, like building a home, or fixing a car. The one time he'd tried to be romantic it had blown up in his face.

He opened the truck door. "Let's get this over with."

MIA DUCKED INTO the Cherry Pit as Will held the door open for her. She hated that he was hurting over Katie. Although frankly he was better off without a woman who slept with another man while keeping Will on a string.

The retro diner had a black and white color scheme with cherry red accents and gave off a welcoming homey vibe. There was a counter with a grill behind it, booths lining the windows and round tables occupying the space in between. The aroma of fresh coffee and frying bacon made her mouth water. From the number of people sipping coffee or tucking into homemade meals, it was clearly a favorite local hangout.

Will stopped inside the door to scan for Katie. "She's not here yet. Let's take that booth in the middle."

Mia slid Billy's car seat inside the banquette and stripped

off her gloves and hat. Will hung their jackets on the hooks at the end of the booth and then sat opposite her.

She picked up a plastic-coated menu from behind the condiments tray. "I didn't have much breakfast. Are the pancakes good?"

"Everything's good here." He drummed his fingers on the Formica table.

She glanced up at him. "Don't let her see you're upset or nervous."

"I'm not." He stopped drumming and took to flipping a sugar packet over and over.

Mia put down the menu and put a hand on his. "Will, look at me."

His troubled blue eyes were rimmed with lashes of old gold. "What?"

"I haven't known you for long but it's very clear to me that you're an amazing guy," Mia told him. "You deserve the best. Do you hear what I'm saying?"

"Well, this is cozy." A Nordic-looking blonde stood at the end of the booth.

"Katie." Will got to his feet and she slid in to take a seat.

Will hesitated then slid in beside Mia. Surprised, she moved over but there was only so far she could go because of Billy's car seat. Will's thigh pressed against hers.

"Got enough room?" He slid his arm along the back of the booth and his fingers brushed her hair, making the back of her neck tingle. "Mia, this is Katie."

Mia smiled. "Will's told me all about you."

"He's negatively biased, given the way things ended." Katie took her time removing her felt hat and leather gloves. All the while her curious gaze checked out Mia. The baby. Will's arm at Mia's back.

"It was all good," Mia assured her. She didn't want to cause a scene, just let Katie know that other people valued Will even if she didn't. "Will's very kind."

"Yes, he is." Katie turned to him. "How was your Christmas? How are your mom and dad?"

"They're good," Will said. "Christmas was…eventful, to say the least."

Mia followed the conversation with interest. Katie was stilted and Will was tense, jiggling his foot. The movement transmitted itself to her leg and she put a hand on his thigh. The jiggling stopped but the tension remained. Gently, she squeezed and he relaxed a little.

"Eventful?" Katie prompted.

Just then the waitress, a petite blonde with a swinging ponytail and name tag that read Skye, bounced up and pulled out her notepad. "Hey, guys. What can I get you?"

"Just coffee," Katie said. "I can't stay long."

Mia gave the menu one last look. "I'll have the Mountain Man breakfast and a hot chocolate."

Katie's eyebrows rose as if to say, "You're not eating for two anymore." Or maybe that was Mia's insecurity talking.

"I'm nursing," she said then kicked herself for feeling she

needed to explain. Her hand tightened on Will's thigh. He covered it with his, returning the moral support.

"Coffee and a blueberry muffin, please," Will said.

Skye cooed over the baby. "Newborns are so darling. When was he born?"

"Christmas morning." Mia beamed. "Will delivered him."

"Excuse me?" Katie's mouth fell open. "Will, you didn't tell me that."

Seriously? Mia frowned. How could she dump the guy and expect him to call and tell her stuff that happened to him?

"Mia got caught in the snowstorm on her way to visit her sister," he explained. "She stumbled into the packing shed on Christmas Eve. Luckily I happened to be in my office."

"Oh, Will, working on Christmas Eve?" Katie's blue eyes were pitying. "Aren't you enjoying the holiday? Remember how your family used to sing Christmas carols?"

"They still do," Mia cut in. Did Katie think everything stopped because she wasn't part of Will's life anymore? "The whole family was together yesterday for carols and a party. It was so fun." *See what you're missing?*

Skye came back with the hot drinks and Will's muffin. "Be right back with your breakfast," she promised Mia.

"Marcus and I went to his parents' house in Vale," Katie said, stirring sweetener into her coffee. "They had a catered cocktail party for a hundred people on Christmas Eve. It took three staff members all afternoon to decorate the twenty-foot tree in their atrium. On Christmas morning we went skiing followed by a sauna."

"Sounds amazing," Will said.

It sounded impersonal and pretentious to Mia, like a party Jared's parents would throw. All glitz and no human warmth. Just like the whopper of a diamond cluster on Katie's ring finger.

"Linda brought over mince tarts." Mia said. "Can't beat homemade."

"I used to love the holidays at your place, Will." Katie reached across and touched his hand. "I miss all the kitschy touches your family go in for."

Piss or get off the pot, Bitch. Beneath the table, Mia squeezed his leg.

Will roughly tore the paper off his muffin, taking half the moist crumb with it. "Your new man and his family will provide other compensations, I'm sure," he said tightly.

"I'm so glad you're okay with this, Will," Katie went on, touching his hand again. "I never wanted to hurt you."

Mia glared into her hot chocolate. The woman was tugging on that string, trying to see if he was still attached.

Skye brought Mia's breakfast—eggs, pancakes, sausages and hash browns with toast on a side plate. "Enjoy."

"Oh, man," Mia said, wondering where to start. "I might need some help with this."

"Just tell me one thing," Will said to Katie, tapping the

table with his forefinger. "If I'd asked you to marry me last Christmas, before you went to Marietta, would you have said yes?"

Katie glanced at Mia. "I don't think this is the right time to talk about that."

"It's now or never," Will said.

"I didn't mean to fall in love with Marcus," Katie said. "It just happened. I know that sounds like a cliché but it literally hit me like a thunderbolt from the blue. Will, I'm sorry, but it felt so different from what we had. If you'd proposed last Christmas I would have said yes—and it would have been a mistake." Distressed, she pushed away her half-finished coffee and rose. "I've got to go."

Mia half expected Will to try and stop her but he didn't, just exchanged the bag he'd brought with hers in silence. Mia concentrated on cutting up her sausage. In her peripheral vision she saw Katie lean in for a stiff embrace and lift her cheek to be kissed.

Another surprise. Will ignored the rebuff and pulled her into a warm hug. "Take care." His voice broke a little.

Mia glanced up in time to see Katie pull away, her eyes shiny. Then Katie grabbed her hat and gloves and the bag containing God knows what mementos, and practically ran for the exit. In that instant, Mia's impression of the other woman did a one-eighty. Katie did care about Will even if she wasn't going to marry him. Damn, now Mia felt sorry for her.

Will slid into the spot Katie had vacated and pulled his coffee across the table to gaze morosely into the foamy depths. "That went well. Not."

Mia started dividing her meal, piling sausages and hash browns on the toast plate along with half her scrambled eggs. "Eat."

"What the hell did she mean, so different to what we had?" Will said bitterly, stabbing at a piece of sausage. "We were long past the hearts and flowers stage but we loved each other."

"An 'on-again, off-again' relationship doesn't sound like you *had* to have her in your life, or else," Mia pointed out gently. "If you were passionately in love and wanted to marry her, wouldn't you have done it years ago?" She shrugged, head tilted. "Just saying."

"Are you suggesting I should have realized long ago that our relationship had run its course and had the guts to end it?" Will demanded.

"No, *you're* saying that." Mia took a bite of egg. "I think she lost you long before she met Marcus and she knew it. Why would she settle for lukewarm when he gave her fireworks? I'm speculating, obviously, but that's what I think."

"I loved her," Will protested. "I was building a house for us to live in."

"Did you consult her about location and the design?"

"She always knew we would live next to the orchard," he

said, then thought a moment. "I guess I made most of the decisions on my own. I knew what I wanted and she didn't seem to care." He winced at the implications of that statement.

"You need to say goodbye to your old vision of your life," Mia suggested.

Will's features tightened. "She should have said if she was unhappy. We could have tried to fix it."

"You heard her: she didn't plan to fall in love with someone else." Mia ached to see this good man hurting. She put a hand on his arm. He looked at her, bewildered. "It's not because you're not lovable. Or…" *Desirable.*

No, she could not say that. But it was true. Will was gorgeous and sexy. And thinking back to when he arrived at the cottage earlier, man, did he smell good. She looked at his mouth and imagined leaning over the table and kissing him. Thinking was almost like doing. Her heart beat faster and her body warmed. Will stared at her oddly, as if she'd spoken the thought aloud. Blushing, she turned to Billy, adjusting his blanket needlessly.

"Is he okay?" Will asked.

"Fine." She made herself breathe, getting oxygen back into her lungs. That moment of heat that flashed between them had *not* happened. Aside from her vow to focus solely on her son and get her life back in order, Will was clearly on the rebound. Everyone knew that falling for someone with unresolved baggage was a recipe for disaster.

Chapter Seven

WILL CARRIED BILLY to the truck, his mind racing. As if he didn't have enough to process with Katie… That look he'd exchanged with Mia—what the hell had that been about? Had he imagined it, or had she felt something, too? No, he must have imagined it. She was a war widow mourning her late husband. And a brand-new mom. She wasn't even thinking about sex or romance with some guy she'd just met. He'd projected his own conflicted feelings on her. Yeah, that was it.

He glanced back to see her peering into the bag of his things Katie had returned. "Are you looking through my stuff?" he asked, more amused than not.

"A comb, a paperback thriller, an old sweater, a Bruce Springsteen CD and a canning jar." Mia's rich dark brown hair billowed out beneath her red cap, her smile teasing. She reminded him of a sparkly eyed Christmas elf. A grown-up, sexy elf. "Is this all of you she collected in ten years?"

"Guess so." Or was that all of himself that he'd given Katie? Had he subconsciously held back for fear that someday they would break up? "She returned the canning jar because my mom likes to refill them and give away more preserves."

"Good to know," Mia said. "I'll remember to give back the jam jar when I'm done."

Will strapped Billy's car seat inside the truck, totally confused over his feelings about Katie. Mia couldn't *know*. What she'd said had to be guesswork, but her observations had rung true and if they were true, he had to bear some responsibility for his failed relationship. Certainly, he and Katie had spent more time apart in the past five years than they had together.

Judging by the way Katie's face lit up when she spoke of Marcus, she really was in love. And Mia's assessment of him and his ex as lukewarm? Ouch. He'd always thought how great it was that they were so relaxed with each other. When had his relationship with Katie turned into no more than a hypothetical vision of the future—marriage, house, couple of kids? When had he traded passion for comfortable?

He opened the front passenger door and Mia climbed in. The elf had a nice ass. *Stop right there. Mia was a no-go zone.* Will got in and started the engine but he didn't pull out. "Thanks for coming with me."

"No worries."

His gaze dropped to her mouth. Her lips looked soft and full. What would they taste like if he kissed her right now? Sweet with maple syrup or dark like chocolate?

"I'm going to miss you," she said unexpectedly.

It hit him that this might be the last time he saw her and Billy. Once she went to her sister's house, it was goodbye Charlie. It felt like another bruise on his already raw heart.

"We'll keep in touch," he said. "Send me photos of Billy. Let me know how he's doing."

"I'll have to—if you're going to be his godfather."

That took him a moment to process then a grin spread across his face. "Really, you want me to be his godfather?"

"Would you?" Her eyebrows lifted hopefully.

The thought of having an active role in Billy's life was something to look forward to and participate in. A continuation of the connection to the child. And the mother. Mia, the flesh and blood woman sitting next to him, was anything but hypothetical.

"Yes, I would," he said. "Absolutely."

"Do you know what a godfather does?" she asked with a bemused smile.

"No, what?"

"I can't tell you off the top of my head but I know it's a big responsibility. If you take it seriously, that is."

"Hey, I'm serious," Will said. "The kid has my baby blanket. Send me the details."

Still grinning, he drove the few blocks to her sister's house. Laney was outside, shoveling a path to her front door. Her light brown ponytail flew as she tossed clumps of snow. Hearing the engine stop, she looked up and waved.

"Do you want to come in?" Mia asked.

Will shook his head. "I'd better keep going."

She leaned in to hug him. He put his arms around her and breathed in the scent of her hair, her skin. Easing back a little she smiled into his eyes. Ignoring the warning bells clamoring in his head he followed his instincts and kissed her lightly on her full, soft lips. The cold tip of her nose hit his cheek and made him smile. The kiss was brief, and very chaste, but a flame burst to life inside. Lukewarm, him? No, definitely not. "See you…next time, whenever that is."

She placed both hands on either side of his face. "Be happy, okay?"

"I am happy." And to his surprise, he was. Somehow in the three days since Christmas Eve a subtle change had taken place inside him. He was looking forward to the New Year, instead of brooding over the old one.

Then Laney banged on Mia's window and Mia opened the door and both women were shrieking and hugging. Will got Billy out of the truck along with Mia's suitcase and carried them both up to the house, wading through the last few feet of snow to wait while Laney opened the door. Laney invited him in, too, but Will thanked her and said no, he had things to do. His gaze met Mia's one last time, lingered a few seconds, then he walked back to his truck, filled with a sense of loss but also of renewal.

It was time to put his house in order.

"SO, TELL ME everything," Laney said, carrying cups of hot chocolate into the snug living room warmly decorated in vintage furniture and colorful bric-a-brac. Her cheeks still glowed pink from shoveling the path. "I was frantic when we got cut off in the middle of your labor."

"You got us through the worst. Will and nature did the rest." Mia moved her hand in light circles over Billy's cheek as he slept in a nest of blankets on the couch beside her. How long would she have to couch surf before she had a home of her own again? She needed to find a job first so she could pay rent but it was too soon to leave Billy. "Have you heard from Mom and Dad?"

"They're excited about the baby. They said to Skype as soon as we were together, no matter what time it was over there." Laney reached for her laptop resting on the wooden chest she used for a coffee table and booted it up. Then she crossed the room to sit next to Mia as the computer dialed.

"Hello?" Mia's mother, Giulia, her short dark hair mussed and curly, sat up in bed with her iPad. "Laney, can you see me? Where are you?"

"I'm at home." Laney turned the screen to include Mia. "Mia's here with her baby."

"Hi, Mom." Mia held up Billy so her mother could see him. "Meet your grandson, Jared William. You can't tell because he's asleep but he has the most beautiful blue eyes."

"*Bello!*" Giulia put a hand to her cheek. Then she shook her husband's shoulder. "Tony, wake up. It's Laney and Mia with her baby."

"What time is it there?" Mia said.

"Nearly five a.m.," Giulia said. "It doesn't matter. We get up early. Hang on, I'm going to move to the dining room."

Mia and Laney got a flashing view of a disheveled double bed, a tiled floor, a hallway and then a wallpapered room crammed with dark furniture. Giulia set the iPad on the table and said she'd be back in a moment. Mia and Laney were left staring at a murky landscape of mountains and lakes.

"Quickly, before they get back, have you told them you lost your job?" Laney asked.

"No, and don't you tell them," Mia said. "They've got enough to worry about with *Nonna*." She sighed. "I'll have to find somewhere new to live, too. My old apartment was too expensive and I let it go."

Their parents appeared, walking slowly on either side of the girls' grandmother, supporting her. *Nonna*, her white hair in a long braid, was wrapped in a dressing gown with a shawl over her stooped shoulders. *Nonna* sat with Giulia next to her. Tony stood behind, leaning down to be visible on the small screen.

"*Ciao, Nonna*," Mia said, shocked to see how frail her grandmother looked compared to when Mia had stayed with her three years ago. "*Come stai?*" How are you?

"*Bene, bene.*" She gestured at the screen and her pale face creased into a smile even as tears appeared in her eyes. "*È un bellissimo bambino. Come si chiama?*"

"What's she saying?" Laney asked.

"He's a beautiful baby. What's his name?" Mia translated. "Jared William Tempesta," she said to her grandmother, raising her voice so she could hear. "*Lo chiamo*, Billy." I call him Billy. "*Buon Compleanno.*" Happy Birthday.

"*Grazie.*" Her *nonna* beamed and said in Italian that she'd had sixty guests at her party. Everyone had brought food and they'd eaten beneath the olive trees on three long tables.

Mia asked after the rest of the family. Conversation continued in both Italian and English—her father updating Mia on her uncle and the winery where Mia had worked for two years, *Nonna* giving details of her hip operation and recovery, and Giulia offering advice on establishing a sleeping pattern for Billy. It was chaotic and disjointed, with her parents and her grandmother arguing and laughing, their hands flying in a digital blur.

Mia did her best to translate for Laney who only spoke a few words of Italian. Mia missed her family and their animated, emotional exchanges. When it came time to say goodbye, she blew her grandmother a kiss, her eyes blurring as her father led the elderly woman back to bed.

"How is *Nonna*, really?" Mia asked her mother. "She

looks so pale."

"The doctors say she's doing really well considering her age," Giulia said. "She can manage a few steps unassisted and will do more in time. Don't worry, darling, soon she'll be making pasta and bossing us all around again."

"How long are you and Dad going to be in Italy?"

"It's hard to say. A couple more weeks, at least. We want to make sure she can manage on her own. Your uncles and aunts do a lot but they're all working or are looking after grandchildren. It's good for *Nonna* to have us here with her full time for now."

"I miss you guys, especially now that I have Billy."

"We miss you, too," Giulia said. "Nothing short of *Nonna*'s accident could have prevented us from being there when your baby was born. How long are you staying with Laney?"

"Till the New Year," Mia replied.

"We'll get back to you on that," Laney said.

Their mother looked from one to the other but didn't pursue it. "How long do you plan to take off work, Mia?"

"I'm not sure," Mia said. "A month probably."

"Does the winery have a maternity leave program?" her mother said. "Three months would be better to allow you to bond with the baby."

"Uh, it could end up being three months," Mia said vaguely. "We should let you go back to bed. I'll call again when it's a better time."

They said their goodbyes and Laney ended the call. The living room seemed quiet after their lively conversation.

"What did you mean we need to talk about my stay?" Mia asked.

Laney went back to her chair, giving Mia room to spread out again with Billy. "My housemate moved out before Christmas so I have a spare room. My friend Shelley can move in but I wanted to offer you the room first."

Mia wiped a speck of dribble away from Billy's mouth with the corner of the blanket. He was sweet and peaceful when he was sleeping but he did cry at times and that would only get worse as he started teething. Or he might get colic like her friend Amy's baby and keep the house up half the night. She would love to stay with Laney but her sister needed to be alert and rested for when she had to go to work as a midwife. As Mia knew only too well, babies were born at all hours of the day and night.

"Thanks, Laney, but Jared's parents are expecting me for an extended visit. They have a huge house and I can stay until I find another job and a place of my own."

"It would be fun to have you here. You should be near family," Laney protested.

"I'd love to, believe me. But Nora and Jed are Billy's family, too. Nora is dying to see him. I…I feel I owe it to them and to Billy." She paused. "And to Jared."

"Oh, him." Laney waved a hand dismissively. Her sister had never made a secret of not liking Jared.

"He was my husband," Mia said quietly. Despite every-thing he'd done, loyalty to Jared's memory had always stopped her from confiding fully in Laney. Gambling was an illness; he couldn't help the way he was. Besides, how would Billy feel when he was older if he heard whispered rumors circulating about things his father had done?

"I thought you didn't like his parents," Laney said.

"I don't *dis*like them," Mia said. "They're just a little controlling."

"Is it about money?" Laney persisted. "I can give you a loan if you need it. I got the impression Jared didn't leave you much."

"I'm fine. But thanks." Again, a thread of anxiety insinu-ated itself. Jared had left her nothing but debts, which she'd paid after his death. "Jared made some investments that didn't pan out but he would have recouped his money if he hadn't been killed."

"Right." There was frank disbelief in Laney's voice. "His insolvency wouldn't have something to do with his trips to Reno, would it?"

"He went there on business," Mia said. "The family is thinking of buying a hotel there."

"You lost your house," Laney pointed out.

"It was too big for me anyway."

"Mia, I'm your sister." Laney crossed to the couch and put her arm around Mia's shoulders. "You can tell me if your marriage wasn't all you hoped it would be."

"There's nothing to tell." Mia pushed herself to her feet and carried their mugs to the kitchen. Laney had warned her not to marry so hastily. She hadn't listened and now she felt a fool. But Jared was dead so what was the point of rehashing?

"Before you met Jared you had a good job, your own apartment, a car and money in the bank," Laney said, following her. "Now all you have is your car."

And she was lucky to have that after paying off Jared's debts.

"Losing my job wasn't Jared's fault," she said. It was scary how quickly a person could lose nearly everything. Scary how she could have trusted him to the point where she'd agreed to let him remortgage the house and borrow money, supposedly to buy an investment property. Instead he'd used the funds to gamble—and lost.

"But losing the house was, right?" Laney persisted.

She leaned on the sink and fought a sudden rush of tears. How long before her damn hormones settled down? The last thing she wanted was conflict with Laney during these few precious days they had together. But she owed her sister some explanation for the way her life had gone downhill this past year.

"He had a gambling problem," Mia admitted, wiping her eyes with a paper towel from the roll on the counter. "And yes, it caused problems between us when we couldn't make mortgage payments." In fact, she'd been ready to leave him for lying to her about something so important as the roof over their heads. Jared had begged her to give him a second chance and reluctantly she'd agreed. "But he was doing something about it. He promised to turn over a new leaf."

"By joining the army?" Laney said skeptically. "He had a responsible, well-paying job. Why didn't he just go to Gambler's Anonymous?"

"He tried that but couldn't stick it," Mia said. "Anyway, he didn't like working for his father. He hoped the army would teach him self-discipline and give him a higher purpose. He set up an account to wire transfer the bulk of his paycheck to me so he couldn't gamble online. That convinced me he was serious about wanting to change."

"Well, maybe he was," Laney said grudgingly. "No one is all bad."

"I know you weren't Jared's biggest fan," Mia said. "But he loved me."

"And did you love him—truly, I mean?" Laney said. "Even knowing his weakness?"

"I...I did." Certainly she had at first. Even later, she'd *wanted* to love him. She'd wanted to salvage her marriage and was willing to give him the benefit of the doubt one more time. The last weekend they'd spent together before he'd shipped off to Iraq had almost been like their honeymoon days, making love night and day, doing crazy things, having fun. "He was spontaneous and exciting."

Why did that make him sound so superficial? Was that

all she could come up with as reason to love him?

"His spontaneity gave you permission to indulge your impulsive streak," Laney pointed out. "Maybe he did love you. Doesn't mean he was good for you. I don't want to hurt you but sisters got to tell it like it is." She wrapped her arms around Mia in a warm hug. "You okay?"

"Of course." Mia wiped her eyes and clung to her for a moment. "How about we kick back and binge watch old movies?"

"I got the box set of *Gilmore Girls* from my friend in Butte," Laney said. "We can work our way through the seasons."

"Perfect." As teenagers she and Laney had never missed an episode. Watching them all again would be fun.

Laney opened a cupboard and brought down snacks. "Chocolate chip cookies or popcorn?"

"Both," Mia said. "I'm full from breakfast but I might be able to nibble. I was seriously junk food deprived in the hospital. Then Will and his family gave me nothing but delicious, healthy food."

"You poor thing," Laney mocked, opening the cookies. "How did you survive?"

"It was touch and go." Mia put the popcorn in the microwave and set the timer. They stood there and watched the bag slowly inflate. "Will's a really a nice guy. Do you know him?"

"Only to see around town. The Starrs are a big family,

lots of cousins. They pioneered this area and between them all they practically own the town." Laney glanced up at her. "Are you interested in him? He's hot."

"Is he?" An involuntary smile came to her lips thinking about his kiss. It hadn't been much more than a peck but she'd felt a tingling warmth. However, she wasn't idiot enough to think about starting something with him. Jared hadn't been dead a year. Regardless of whether she loved her late husband or not, she wasn't ready. And yet, that kiss…

"What are you smiling about?" Laney nudged her. "Will?"

"I'm not interested in dating." Mia felt her cheeks heat. "I just gave birth for God's sake. I'm not ready for another man. Not sure I will ever be."

Knowing Laney's matchmaking tendencies, she needed to make that very clear. Before she got involved with anyone else—if she ever did again—she needed to focus on getting her life back on track. She had Billy to look after now.

"You're way too young to say that," Laney said. "Will Starr is a catch. You could do a lot worse."

"Which is precisely why I couldn't hook up with him, even if I was interested," Mia said. "I'm in a position of weakness—no money, no job, no status. If I ever do fall in love again it won't happen until I'm solvent." God forbid he think she was looking for "a good catch" as Laney put it. "I don't want to be saved by a man. I can save myself, thank you very much."

"Of course you can," Laney said. "But he kissed you in the truck. I saw so don't try to deny it."

"It was just a goodbye kiss," Mia said. Although that's not how it had felt to her. More like a *Hello! Where have you been all my life?* kiss. With a little, *Stay tuned, more to come*, thrown in. "I asked him on impulse to be Billy's godfather," she confessed. "I didn't even stop to think. I just blurted it out. Was that stupid?"

"Hell, I don't know," Laney said. "Did he agree?"

Mia nodded. "He was so great at the birth. He really bonded with Billy. And…"

If he was godfather they would have to stay in touch. She wasn't looking for anything romantic but couldn't she like him as a friend? That thought made her circle around to the kiss again. Definitely not the kiss of a friend.

"And…?" Laney prompted suggestively.

"If I wasn't a widow and a new mother with post-baby body issues and out of control hormones, I might be interested," Mia admitted, trying to make light of the discussion.

"I knew it," Laney said triumphantly.

The microwave beeped. Mia pulled out the bag and poured hot, buttery popcorn into a bowl.

"But it's not going to happen," she said. "He's just been dumped by his so-called girlfriend. He's angry and hurt and still in love with her. Rebound relationships never last. It's a known fact." She offered the bowl to Laney. "New Year's resolution—I'm going to work on curbing my impulsiveness."

Laney took a handful of popcorn and started munching. "Like when you drove here with a snowstorm forecast and you were shortly to give birth?"

"I thought I could beat the weather. Can I help it if both the blizzard and the baby came early?" Mia hip checked her. "Are we going to stand around and yak all day or are we going to watch Lorelai and Rory do it?"

"Lorelai and Rory," Laney said. "They talk faster."

Mia followed her back into the living room. For all she knew Will might still get back together with Katie. Or supposing, hypothetically, that Mia did go out with him, he could work through his relationship problems with her and then move on to another woman. She didn't need that kind of emotional drama in her life.

But as she settled in front of the TV, she couldn't help but wonder what Will was doing right now. Was he thinking about Katie?

Or about her?

Chapter Eight

Six weeks later…

WILL SET THE paint roller in the tray and stepped back to survey his bedroom walls. Warm white walls with semi-gloss trim might not be the most creative color scheme but he wanted something he wouldn't get tired of in a year. Once he bought more furniture and hung pictures and added personal items he'd picked up over the years, it would look better.

He washed the paint tray and roller in the laundry room and stuck the brushes into a jar of water then scrubbed his hands. Back in the kitchen he stuck half a leftover pizza in the microwave and foraged in the fridge for something vaguely green and healthy. He sniffed at the supermarket mixed salad and decided it was edible.

Idly scrolling through his phone he found Mia had sent a new photo of Billy. The baby's thick swatch of black hair had fallen out and been replaced by light brown fluff that showed signs of a wave. Billy's eyes had changed color, too, turning from the slate blue of a newborn to warm amber like

Mia's.

Will texted back, attaching a funny meme of a baby and a puppy that Mia would get a kick out of, as well as updated photos of his newly painted house. He kept their interactions light but behind every exchange was the memory of their fleeting kiss in his truck as they said goodbye. At least, he thought about the kiss. No doubt she simply saw him as a friend—and Billy's godfather.

Grabbing his reheated pizza, he perched on a barstool and read the rest of his messages. Garret wanted to know if he was coming to the basketball game in Polson; Cody sent a photo from the rodeo in Texas where he was bronco riding; Alex passed along a possible new market for cherries in Dubai.

Katie sent an invitation to her and Marcus's wedding.

Will stopped chewing and waited for the sick feeling of bitterness and resentment. It didn't come. The question continued to nag him—had he ever loved Katie passionately? Their youthful heady days of infatuation had eased into a comfortable friendship over time. He suspected Mia was right: if he and Katie had truly been in love they would have married a long time ago. Katie wouldn't have traveled and stayed away so long and neither of them would have gone out with other people. It had taken Katie's engagement, and then Mia's off the cuff assessment to get him to see it. Now that he did, he wondered why it had taken him so long to realize the truth.

The weight of his own expectations along with those of his and Katie's families and friends had led him to believe their marriage was a foregone conclusion. He'd never felt a sense of urgency about the prospect, just a quiet contentment and a feeling of inevitability. Katie really had saved them from a big mistake. What he felt for her now was gratitude and a wish for her happiness. His mother had said he was on the rebound but he wasn't dating, desperately trying to fill the gap that Katie had left. Finishing his house was his most urgent and fulfilling task.

He flipped out of messages and into his photo gallery. Seeing Mia holding up Billy next to her cheek made him smile. She was a woman he could really fall for but she wasn't available emotionally. He hated that she was still hurting over the death of her late husband. How long before the pain faded and she could feel joy again? He hesitated, then googled how long it took to get over the death of a much-loved partner. The blog he landed on posted heart-wrenching accounts of grief that weren't encouraging. Some women—and it was mostly women who posted—had been mourning their husbands and boyfriends for years. Will closed the site after reading only a few posts, feeling ghoulish and sad.

Well, he wasn't pursuing Mia anyway. Falling for her would be dumb on so many levels he couldn't even count them. He just wished he didn't think of her twenty times a day.

His phone chimed, announcing a new message, and he toggled back to that screen. It was Mia, inviting him to Billy's christening. Without even looking at the date or location he started typing yes. He hit send and seconds later, she called.

"Hi, Will." She sounded breathless. Either she'd been running or she was nervous. "I just got your reply. That's great you can make it."

"Wouldn't miss it." His voice didn't sound any too steady either. He cleared his throat. "How's the babe?"

"Billy's great. He turns his head when he hears my voice and he's holding his head up all by himself. He's so cute."

"I can't wait to see him in person." He paused. "How are you doing?"

"Terrific!" she said, her voice overly bright. "Nora and Jed are so generous. Nora buys baby stuff before I even realize Billy needs it."

Will had gotten into the habit on Mia's rare phone calls of trying to read between the lines. He'd gained the impression that she sometimes covered up her true feelings. Right now, he wasn't buying her enthusiasm. Nora and Jed sounded too good to be true.

"I'm sure they're fine people," he said noncommittally. "I look forward to meeting them."

"Since you're godfather, you're supposed to stand at the font with me while Billy's baptized," Mia said. "Are you okay with that?"

Delivering Billy had been momentous. Being invited to be godfather at the christening was almost as huge. Mia was publicly declaring that Will was part of Billy's life. It meant a lot to him. "I'd be honored."

"Laney will be there as his godmother. I suggested to her that you two could drive down together but she's going to stop in Butte on her way back to see her friend."

"If that falls through, she can come with me." Will paused then changed the subject. "How's the job search going?"

"How's your house coming?" Mia said at the same time.

"I finished painting today," he replied. "Next week the guys come to lay the hardwood floor in the living room and hallway. Week after that the carpet layers do the bedrooms. Then I can start moving furniture in. It's coming together."

"I'd love to see it," she said.

"Drive up for the weekend." There was silence. He kicked the cupboard door with his sock foot and winced at the stab of pain to his big toe. "Forget it. Dumb idea. And the jobs?"

"Nothing yet." Frustration tinged her voice. "Billy keeps me pretty busy so it's hard to find the time to apply. Everything's online these days and I individually tailor every application. It's taking forever. But I'll get there."

He walked to the window where he could just see the roof of the cottage over the treetops. It didn't seem that long ago she'd stayed there. "My friends Stewart and Kristin own a winery in Sweetheart and are looking for someone to work in their cellar door. They can't offer full time until summer but I thought you might be interested."

"Thanks but I'm looking in the Billings area first. Nora said she'll watch Billy three days a week." Mia gave a dry laugh. "That's code for she'll hire a nanny but at least Billy can be at home and I can go to work. I'm grateful to have their help and at the same time look forward to the day I don't need it anymore."

"Okay. Just thought I'd mention it." It would have been nice if she lived in Sweetheart but maybe that would be harder for him to be around her and knowing he couldn't have her. Even so, he added, "Let me know if you change your mind."

"Thank you, Will. I can never repay you for everything you've done for me."

"You already have." It was true. Whether it was due to the jolt of witnessing the birth or being inspired by Mia's gutsy approach to life, or her insights into his relationship with Katie, he'd come out of his slump.

His father's truck was bumping down the lane, reminding him he and the old man had a date to overhaul the tractor they used to pull the flatbed with cherry containers during picking season. "I've got to go but I'll see you soon. Give Billy a hug from me." His voice softened. "Take care."

"You, too." Mia paused. "Billy hugs you back."

Will put the phone down with a wry smile. As much as

he would love to give Billy a cuddle, he'd prefer a hug from Mia. He checked the date on the invitation. Two weeks. He would see her then.

His smile faded. He and Mia were just friends. He had a responsibility to her son to be there for him. He'd looked up the duties of godfather and basically the modern interpretation meant he was supposed to remember birthdays and Christmas, be a mentor to guide and advise and at the same time be the 'fun uncle' that allowed a little sanctioned mischief without going overboard.

He was more than fine with all that. But if he pursued Mia and she rejected him for some reason like oh, say, being in love with her dead husband, then the potential tension could impact his future relationship with Billy. If Will was going to take his role as godfather seriously he needed to not get involved with the mom.

MIA, LYING ON Jared's old bed, hung up after talking to Will. A model of a WWII Spitfire spun gently on fishing line above her head. What Nora had created here wasn't just a shrine to her son's memory but a time capsule of Jared from the ages of ten to twenty when he'd moved out on his own. Sporting trophies and pennants, posters of hot cars and football players, pinups of Beyoncé and Mila Kunis, CDs, souvenirs of Hawaii, Reno, Las Vegas and New York, his framed degree from business school, et cetera et cetera.

It was claustrophobic.

"I'll put you in here," Nora had said when Mia arrived the day after New Year's. Nora with her perfectly coiffed auburn hair and sleek pantsuit. "You'll feel close to him. I always do. Sometimes I like to sit on the bed and look at his things and remember." When Mia raised her eyebrows, Nora had added quickly, "Don't worry, I won't come in while you're here."

But Mia suspected she did. Often she came home from visiting her parents to find an imprint on the quilt. Nothing was touched—Mia didn't worry that Nora snooped through her things—but it was sad and tragic and just a little creepy. She'd had to bite her tongue not to tell Will everything about her situation but after a couple of months at Nora and Jed's she was climbing the walls. Worse, colluding in the deification of Jared Richards was eating away at her insides.

Her parents had offered to put her and Billy up until she could afford her own place but they'd downsized the previous year to a one-bedroom apartment. The weekend she'd spent with them after they'd returned from Italy—while it had been wonderful to see them—had convinced all concerned that cramming three adults and a newborn into a small living space wasn't a great idea.

Her occasional phone calls to Will were her lifeline to sanity. Even though she knew she was playing with fire sometimes she just had to hear his voice and be brought down to earth by his calm, rational good humor. Many times she wanted to call but didn't, putting it off until she was desperate, otherwise she'd be calling every day.

Thank goodness he'd agreed to stand up at the font with her. With Laney on her other side, her parents in the congregation, along with her college friends, she would be buffered from the Richards family and their legion of society acquaintances.

She couldn't wait to see Will. After she and Laney had binged on *Gilmore Girls* they'd had watched old movies, including *Cat On A Hot Tin Roof.* The young Paul Newman with his blue bedroom eyes and knowing grin reminded her so much of Will that her sexual fantasies had gone into overdrive.

Stop. Right. There. Just because she hadn't had sex in nearly a year didn't mean she was prepared to screw up her life for a roll in the hay. She had goals. Find a job, her own apartment, provide a stable life for Billy. Anyway, as if Will would want her post-baby body. He might be on the rebound but he wasn't desperate. In fact, she'd be surprised if he wasn't dating someone already.

She dragged herself off the bed and sat at the desk to do her banking. She went over the latest credit card statement alongside her receipts, ticking off items on the list, making sure she hadn't been charged for something she hadn't bought. Then she pored over her dwindling bank statement, looking for ways to cut costs. What she needed to do was prepare a budget for the coming months based on an assumed wage, setting aside so much for food and gas, et cetera, to try to predict when she would be able to move out on her own. Until she actually got a job it was all theoretical but it would make her feel like she was doing something.

She opened the top drawer, searching through scattered pens and paperclips for a calculator. Jared's old mobile phone was tucked in there, along with his dog tags and Oakley sunglasses. After he'd died, she'd been too upset to keep his personal effects and had given them to Nora. Now Mia picked up his phone. Maybe it was the time to finally reread their last few exchanges.

She found her charger and plugged in the phone. She wasn't sure what the point was unless to remind her when she felt angry at the mess Jared had left her in, that what she'd told Laney was true—he had loved her.

Once the phone booted up and gained enough charge, she logged into his messages using the password she knew as well as her own and scrolled through, looking for his posts to her. She came across a name she didn't recognize as one of his many friends. Who was Tiffany?

Mia clicked on the name and brought up a brief exchange.

Tiff, shipping out Mon. Meet me before I go. Make a soldier happy. J

What the? Troubled, Mia read on for Tiffany's reply.

Denver, 3 p.m. We'll do all our favorite dirty things. T xxxx
Wear the lace corset I got you in Vegas.

Tiffany replied with a sexy woman emoji.

Cold ran down Mia's neck and raised the fine hairs on her arms. The last shred of affection she felt for Jared frayed into nothing. The one thing—*the one thing*—she'd clung to was that for all his faults, Jared had at least been faithful. She felt sick to her stomach as she recalled how he'd left for Iraq a day early, telling her that he'd received new orders by email. She'd driven him to the airport herself. It had never occurred to her to check the destination printed on his ticket. That very morning he'd made love to her and promised to be a better man.

Then he'd flown to Denver to meet this Tiffany person.

"Mia, are you here?" Nora knocked once and opened the door. She wore a navy wool dress with a narrow belt and held Billy in her arms. "Look who I found awake in his crib." She spoke gaily but there was the teeniest note of reproach in her voice.

Mia thrust the phone at her, too angry to mince her words. "He was screwing around on me."

Nora's face paled as she read the messages. "Jared was going off to war. You can't judge him."

"I damn well can judge him! Did you know about her?" Mia couldn't even bring herself to say the woman's name.

"Tiffany was an old girlfriend." Nora clicked off the phone and replaced it on the desk. "I didn't know he was still seeing her." She didn't sound convincing.

Mia threw up her hands. She should have known it was pointless to expect Nora to take her side against her golden boy.

Billy began to fret. Mia held out her arms. She'd heard his wakeful babbling sounds in the nursery and left him on purpose, wanting to see how long he could lie there happy. Now she needed the comfort of holding him. "Come to Mamma, baby."

"I'll change him first," Nora said. Billy began to cry.

Mia felt her breasts let down and rose, saying firmly, "I'd better nurse him before I leak."

"All right." Nora handed Billy to her reluctantly.

"Shh, Billy boy," Mia soothed as she worked to free her nursing bra. "It's okay."

"Oh, poor darling," Nora crooned in a baby voice. "Is your mommy pinching you?"

Mia gritted her teeth. Did she have to say that every single time Billy cried? She knew Nora meant it as a joke but it played into her mother's guilt by implying she must be doing something wrong. Billy latched on and she sighed in relief as his sucking eased the pressure on her breasts. Keeping him on the breast, she carried him next door to the nursery.

Mia sat in the rocking chair to nurse. She palpated her breast and frowned. They seemed less full than a week ago. Billy didn't seem to be feeding as often.

"Something wrong?" Nora asked, following her.

"I'm worried my milk is drying up. Billy didn't wake up for his early morning feed today. He didn't yesterday, either." She felt his forehead with the back of her hand. "I hope he's not sick."

"Oh, that," Nora said. "I gave him a bottle."

"What?" She spoke so sharply that Billy wrenched his mouth off her nipple and gazed up at her in alarm. "Why would you do that? You know I want to breastfeed."

Nora clasped her hands in front of her, twisting the many rings on her thin fingers. "You were up so late with him the night before. I wanted to let you sleep."

Mia struggled to keep her voice even. "Being tired is part of being a new mother. If you give him bottles then I produce less milk."

"Is that so bad?" Nora said, then added brightly, "Look what I got at the store for him today. I saw it in the window and couldn't help myself." She spread her arms, gesturing to a miniature car, the kind that a toddler sat on and pushed around with his feet. "Ta-da."

Mia's heart sank at yet another extravagant gift. The plastic hood ornament was the double R of a Rolls Royce. Only the best for Jared's son. "It's super cute, Nora, but way too old for Billy. He's not even crawling yet."

"Oh, that doesn't matter." Nora flapped a hand. "It'll be here when he wants it."

"Thank you. You really shouldn't have though." Mia surveyed the room full of brand-new baby gear with a mixture of resentful gratitude and dismay.

Nora had thought of everything. The crib of polished maple complete with sheets and blankets, filled with stuffed toys. The change table, diaper bag, buggy that converted to a stroller. Everything was top of the line, expensive and in many cases designer. Nora's generosity was overwhelming but the mountain of baby things made Mia want to cry. She'd looked forward to shopping for Billy herself.

Yet how could she complain without appearing ungrateful? Nora knew Mia didn't have much money and this was her way of helping without making Mia feel like a charity case. It hadn't worked though. Mia felt like the poor relation. Nora and Jed paid for everything, not allowing her to contribute to food or utilities even though they'd increased their internet download capacity so she could more easily look online for jobs. They were doing it for Jared's sake, they said, and she would have felt churlish to refuse. But it bothered her…a lot.

If Nora and Jed had been like this with Jared when he was growing up, no wonder he'd acted so entitled. She didn't like to speak ill of the dead but just once she wished her in-laws would acknowledge that Jared hadn't been perfect. Quite the opposite, in fact. But even when confronted with evidence of him having an affair, Nora refused to hear a word against him. Unbelievable.

"We don't want to spoil Billy." Mia breathed slowly and deeply, trying to relax and let her milk flow. "Jared got everything he wanted and I'm not sure it did him good."

Nora's lips pinched together below her long thin nose. "Jared was a wonderful, wonderful man. People misunderstood him."

"Misunderstood? Is that what dishonesty is called these days?" Words she'd kept pent up for months poured out. "He told me he was buying an investment property and he took out a massive second mortgage on our house. Then he gambled the money away." *How much had he spent on Tiffany?* "To make matters worse, he quit his job and went into the army at a much lower rate of pay."

"He didn't quit. Jed fired him," Nora huffed. "If Jed hadn't done that my son might be alive today."

"What?" Mia said, frowning. "Why did Jed fire him?"

"Oh, you know." Nora paced, twisting her rings. "Jared borrowed from the hotel accounts. It wasn't that much and he was going to pay it back."

"He embezzled hotel takings?" Mia pressed a hand over her mouth. Just when she thought she'd plumbed the depths of Jared's misdeeds, it got worse. Not only a mistress but actual criminal activity, too.

"It's in the past," Nora said, dismissing further discussion. "Now, have you sent out the invitations to the christening yet?"

Mia blinked at the sudden change of subject—though she should be used by now to Nora's habit of deflecting uncomfortable topics. The embossed print invitations had sat in a pile on the kitchen counter along with a list of names and addresses for the past three days. "I sent out email invitations this morning and I posted on Facebook."

Nora smiled in that overly indulgent way that meant she was displeased. "My dear, many of my friends, and Jared's aunts and uncles, won't see a notice on social media."

Mia hadn't deliberately avoided writing out a hundred invitations but she had a deadline on a couple of job applications. "I'll get to it tonight."

"Good. My friends have been waiting to hear." Nora started to leave and then paused. "Oh, and Jed will stand up at the altar with you in lieu of Jared. He and I talked about it last night and we agreed that he would be more appropriate than Uncle Lester or one of Jared's friends."

"Thanks, Nora, but my sister Laney, and Will, the man who delivered Billy, are going to stand up with me." Mia kept her tone light but determined. Her heart beat fast as she waited for her mother-in-law to process this unwelcome information. She'd given way on so many things but on this point she had no intention of budging.

"Your sister makes sense but this Will person... You don't really know him," Nora argued. "Wouldn't it be better to have a family member, someone who cares about Billy and will be present in his life?"

"Will cares. He's Billy's godfather," Mia said firmly. "He is going to be part of my son's life."

"I see." Nora's lips compressed and her narrow nostrils

flared. "Jed will be terribly disappointed but if that's what you want…"

"I don't want Jed to be disappointed," Mia began then stopped, not wanting to get dragged into another of those un-winnable discussions she seemed to have with Nora. She took a deep breath and forced a placating smile. "Jed could take photos from your vantage point in the front pew." Jed was a good amateur photographer and specialized in portraits, as the many photos of Jared on the walls of his room attested to. "We could make an album."

"He'd be pleased to do that," Nora acknowledged grudgingly. "By the way, I invited the pastor so we could go over the ceremony. He'll be here shortly. Maybe you could change out of that sweatshirt?"

"Of course." Mia's smile felt like a grimace as she transferred Billy to her other breast.

Nora, having gotten the last word, left. Finally. Mia laid her head back on the carved back of the rocking chair, fighting tears.

She had to get out of here.

Chapter Nine

WILL PULLED INTO the cathedral parking lot in Billings and reached for the gifts wrapped in baby blue paper and tied with a silver ribbon. One was a boxed set of Thomas The Tank Engine books, the other an expensive bottle of scotch to be opened on Billy's twenty-first birthday. Will planned to be there to raise a glass with him.

Turning up his collar against the cold wind, he stepped across the slushy pavement in his good leather shoes and joined the guests funneling up the steps to the carved wooden doors of the massive stone church. There were maybe two hundred people here, a testament to the Richards family's standing in Billings. And no doubt to Mia, herself. She was gutsy, warm-hearted and sweet. She was going to make a great mom. Correction, she already was a great mom.

A painfully thin auburn-haired woman in a mink jacket and a portly gray-haired man in a cashmere overcoat stood on one side of the open carved wooden doors, greeting guests with smiles.

Laney stood on the opposite side, shivering in a blazer

over her maroon wool dress. "Will!"

"Hi, Laney." Will turned gratefully to her familiar face. "How's Mia?"

Laney gave him a quick hug. "She's so happy you agreed to come."

"I wouldn't miss it." Will turned to the auburn haired woman, figuring she must be Mia's mother-in-law. "Hello," he said extending a hand. "I'm Will Starr."

"Nora Richards, Jared Junior's grandmother," she said with a smile that didn't reach her watchful eyes. "This is my husband, Jed."

Jed gripped his hand, squeezing hard. "Nice to meet you. How do you know our Mia?"

Jared Junior? What a handle to stick a baby with. Our Mia? Will hadn't known Mia long but after going through the birth with her, he felt protective of her. "I'm Billy's godfather," he said, staking a counterclaim. "I delivered him."

"Oh, you're that Will." Nora's smile became as icy as the wind that whipped around their ankles. "Welcome." She turned to the next guest coming up the steps.

He was starting to understand the undercurrents in Mia's voice when she talked about her in-laws. He turned back to Laney. "Where is Mia?"

"In an anteroom with Billy." She linked her arm in his and whispered, "Now that you're here, I can escape the Dragon Lady." To Nora and Jed, she said, "Excuse us. The priest wants to give us instructions about the ceremony."

Will and Laney wove their way through the guests waiting to be seated and up the outside of the rows of pews to a door set in a recess in the stone wall. Laney knocked and went in.

In the richly wood-paneled room, Mia bent over Billy's car seat placed on a desk. Her wrap dress in a deep royal blue accentuated her breasts and hips and her billowing hair had been tamed into shiny dark waves around her shoulders. As they entered she glanced up. Wow. He'd thought Mia was beautiful before but seeing her after a few months apart, suddenly she wasn't just a mom. She was a woman.

He must have been staring because her cheeks turned pink. She picked up Billy, arranging the folds of his lacy white christening gown.

"You look amazing." He rested his hand casually on her shoulder as he bent to smile at Billy, angelically nestled in the crook of Mia's arm. The baby regarded Will solemnly. Will tickled him. "Cheer up, kid, you'll be out of the dress and back into pants in no time."

Billy's cheeks creased in a sudden smile that curled his Cupid's bow mouth and crinkled his eyes. Will tickled again and the baby laughed, a tiny chortle.

"Did you hear that laugh?" Will exclaimed.

"That's his first laugh," Mia said, looking stunned. "Not for his mommy who nurses him and walks him when he cries, but you. That's..." She trailed off, lost for words.

"Ah, he's probably laughing at me being dressed up in a suit." Will couldn't stop grinning. Even if it was a coincidence that Billy had laughed for the first time when he was there, he'd witnessed it and that was special.

Mia tickled Billy. "Come on, sweetie, laugh for Mommy."

Laney got into the act, making funny faces. "Hey, hon, it's your Aunty Laney. How about a giggle?"

Will pulled Billy's foot gently in its knitted bootie. "Women are pretty silly, aren't they, buddy?" Billy waved a tiny fist and smiled. "You and I are going fishing, just as soon as you're old enough to hold a rod."

The priest, a young man with a shiny balding head and a red-cheeked round face, entered the room. "The godparents?" he asked, looking at Will and Laney.

Mia nodded and made the introductions. "Laney Tempesta and Will Starr. Father Michael."

"This fine fellow must be Jared William," Father Michael said, solemnly shaking the baby's hand.

"I call him Billy," Mia said. "I'd like him to be referred to by that name, please."

"No problem. Let's go over the ceremony." Father Michael proceeded to outline who would stand where, and when they were to respond.

They filed into the church and up to the baptismal font. Mia stood in front with Billy, next to Father Michael. Will and Laney stood behind and a little to the side. Excited whispers ran through the guests. Then Father Michael began to speak and the church became quiet.

The ceremony wasn't in Latin, which was a relief to Will. Even so he found it hard to concentrate on the words with Mia right in front of him with the light shining on her hair. Next to him, Laney discreetly dabbed at her eyes. Was she thinking, as he was, that Mia looked very brave standing there without her husband? Seeing her straight spine and square shoulders made Will even more determined to be a good godfather to her son.

Funny how babies, even one that wasn't his own, made a man think about the future, something he hadn't done since he'd mapped out his goals after leaving college ten years ago. Life had been simple then—manage the cherry orchard and grow the business. Get the teen boys basketball team he coached to the state finals. Settle down with Katie and raise some kids. He'd thought he was making progress on all fronts until Katie had blindsided him. Now that marriage was off the table it made him question everything else. He was thirty-two years old and he'd never been to Europe, or gone skydiving or learned karate. Was life passing him by?

Billy cried out when Father Michael poured water over his forehead and Mia rocked him quiet. Will, following the priest's prompts, promised to be there for Billy, to celebrate the high points of his godchild's life and be a support and help during the low moments. To offer advice and be a good example of a life well lived. It was a lot to live up to.

Laney made the same promises. The church choir began to sing a hymn and the congregation rose. Mia turned and her brilliant, beautiful smile included him in her circle of family. His chest swelled at the pact he'd just made and how it put into perspective his concerns. Life wasn't about how many places you saw or experiences you had or how much money you made. It was about the people who mattered to you.

The reception was held at Nora and Jed's house in an exclusive neighborhood. Will parked down the broad, tree-lined street and walked up the long drive to the three-story red brick dwelling with ivy growing around mullioned windows. A maid took his coat and he stamped the snow off his shoes before entering a spacious hall that flowed into a large drawing room to the left. Off to the right a broad staircase led up to a second-floor gallery.

Mia, still holding Billy, was surrounded by a steady stream of people coming up to see the baby. Will had no hope of getting close to her and his plan to take her out for a cup of coffee seemed naive in hindsight. He accepted a glass of champagne from the tray of a passing waiter and sipped it slowly to make the one drink last. The roads were still icy through the mountains.

"I'm Giulia, Mia's mother." An attractive woman in her early fifties with wavy dark hair beamed at him and shook his hand vigorously. "I'm so happy to meet you. Mia pointed you out when we were leaving the church. I've wanted to call and thank you but Mia said to wait till the christening. She doesn't like to bother you. I didn't think you would mind but she said no, so I waited." Giulia gestured eloquently. "I always do what Mia says."

"Good to meet you, too." Will laughed, a little bowled over by the stream of words. "I can see where Mia gets her good looks from. How is her grandmother?"

"She's much better, thank you," Giulia said warmly. "Seeing Mia's baby on Skype helped her recovery, I'm positive. Where's Tony? I want you to meet my husband. Tony, come here." She beckoned to an olive-skinned man with graying black hair in a dark brown suit. "Meet Will, the man who delivered Billy. He gave our grandson his name."

"*Ciao*, pleased to meet you." Tony shook hands so hard he sloshed the glass of scotch in his other fist. "Mia told us all about how you delivered Billy. She was lucky you were there. She said how nice your family were to her. Better than…" With a sour look, he lifted his chin in the direction of Jared's parents flanking Mia in the receiving lineup.

"Shh," Giulia said, glancing around. "Mia never says anything bad about Nora and Jed."

"She doesn't need to," Tony said. "You can tell when people aren't nice. Look how they make her show off the baby to every person, like he's a new car or something."

Will glanced over at Mia and frowned. Behind her unfaltering smile, the strain of the day was showing. Billy was fretting, his forehead puckered and his mouth working.

"She's tired."

"They won't let her sit down." Giulia clucked her tongue. "I suggested Mia take a seat and Nora said it was only a little longer. She's been on her feet for hours."

"I'll get her out of there." Will edged his way through the throng to get to Mia, ignoring the huffs and murmured comments. "Excuse me but Mia needs a break." Gently, he took Billy out of her arms and led her through the crowd toward the staircase, ignoring Nora's protests. As they passed a circulating waiter, he said, "A mug of hot Ovaltine to the nursery, please."

"Yes, sir." The waiter went off in the opposite direction.

Across the room, Tony gave him a thumbs-up.

"There is a nursery, I hope?" Will asked Mia.

"Yes, fourth room down the gallery." She held on to the bannister as she climbed the steps.

Nora scurried after them and took hold of Will's jacket sleeve. "Who do you think you are, dragging her and Jared Junior away like that?"

"I'm *Billy's* godfather," he said pleasantly but firmly. "I just promised on a Bible to look after his best interests. I don't mean to be rude but Mia needs to rest and Billy looks like he's hungry."

Right on cue, Billy began to cry. Will had no idea what to do with a crying baby but he held the little guy up to his shoulder and patted his back.

"Sorry, Nora, but he's right," Mia said. "I'll be down in a

little while."

"Make sure you are," Nora said. "And bring Billy even if you have to carry him in his bassinet. Not everyone has had a chance to hold him."

"He's not a football to be passed around," Will said. "I'm sure you can make her excuses. Oh, and please ask the kitchen for a sandwich for Mia to go with her hot drink."

Nora, thankfully, was speechless in the face of this insubordination.

Will put his hand on Mia's back and together they continued to the nursery.

Mia made for the rocking chair. Moving aside her top she put the baby to her breast. At the sound of Billy feeding lustily, Will headed for the door to give her privacy. Women nursing their babies didn't normally affect him one way or another but this was Mia and her breasts held a different kind of interest to him. Getting a free look didn't seem right. "I'll go see how your food and drink are coming along."

"Come back, okay?" Mia said.

"Of course." He paused in the doorway. "Is Nora always like that?"

"She's still grieving." Mia sighed heavily. "She's been very generous to me. All this baby stuff came from her."

"I'm sorry for her loss but... Oh, never mind." Will closed the door behind him. It seemed to him that Mia was the generous one to be so forgiving of her mother-in-law. Having met Nora it made him wonder if Jared was really as wonderful as he sounded. Although, why wouldn't he be? A woman like Mia could have her pick of men.

In the kitchen, caterers and waiters bustled to and fro. Nora watched with an eagle eye, inspecting platters of food going out. Will leaned against the table in the breakfast nook and checked his phone messages to keep out of the way while Mia's tray was prepared.

When she was done annoying the harried caterers, Nora came over to him. "You didn't need to come down here. I would have brought the tray up."

Will put his phone away. "I don't mind."

"She's being well taken care of, you know."

"I can see that," Will said diplomatically. "I only want what's best for her and Billy."

"Is that true?" Nora asked. "Or are you interested in her for yourself?"

He couldn't answer that truthfully so he kept quiet.

"She's still very much in love with her husband," Nora went on. "I hear her crying in his room at night when she thinks no one is listening."

His heart took a hit at this confirmation of what he'd suspected. Even though nearly a year had passed since Mia's husband had died he knew it could take a lot longer than that to get over a beloved partner, if ever. To think of her all alone and sad made his own heart hurt.

"I'm her friend, that's all," Will said. "I'll continue to help her as long as she wants me to."

It wasn't as simple as that, of course. It was true that she aroused his protective instincts but if he was honest, he was attracted to her. He had been even when she was pregnant and even after giving birth when she was still big and ungainly. There was a light in her eyes that drew him, a sparkle in her laughter that lifted his spirits. And something else that he couldn't put his finger on, a spark of chemistry that wasn't just physical but held an emotional connection that made him want to drop everything and be with her. And until Mia told him to go away no Dragon Lady could stop him from coming back.

"I hope that's true," Nora said. "Mia is very special and I don't want her hurt."

"We have that in common, at least." Will returned her hard look with one of his own. "I'll take the tray up."

He knocked to let Mia know he was coming in. She'd changed Billy's diaper and was buttoning him into a onesie that looked like farmer's overalls over a long-sleeved T-shirt.

She passed him to Will, along with a soft, clean cloth. "Can you burp him while I eat?"

"Sure." Will struggled to get a grip on the soft, wriggly baby. "Have you had this kid checked out to make sure he has a skeleton?"

"Sit and lay him over your knee," Mia instructed around a mouthful of turkey sandwich. "Oh, this tastes good. I couldn't eat breakfast I was so nervous about the christening."

Will laid the cloth over his thigh and put Billy down on his tummy, holding him in place while he gingerly patted his back. "Am I doing this right? He's not burping."

"You're fine. Give him a few minutes." Mia rested her head against the high back of the rocking chair and shut her eyes. "I didn't even realize how tense I was until you got me away from the party."

Will let her sleep, if that's what she was doing. The shadows under her eyes suggested her nights were wakeful. "Are you keeping your mommy awake?" he said softly to Billy, making circles with his fingers on the baby's back.

Billy burped loudly and a ribbon of drool wet the cloth. He kicked his legs vigorously, then began to fuss.

Will folded the cloth and shifted it and the baby to his shoulder. Then he got up and walked around the room, jiggling Billy while making sure to keep a hand support his neck. He continued to speak softly. "Any more wind in there, get it out. You've had a big day and it's probably time for your nap. Your mom needs a nap, that's for sure."

Mia also needed to get out of this gilded cage as soon as possible before Nora ground her down. Who cared if she'd bought all this fancy stuff? Probably half of it wasn't even necessary. The kid would grow up spoiled rotten.

"You know, kid, you smell pretty good." Will covertly breathed in the baby scent of the warm snuggly body. Ah, hell, any minute he'd start clucking like a broody hen.

"He's asleep," Mia said, yawning.

Will peered sideways. Billy's eyes were closed and his tiny fists were clenched next to his round cheeks where his head rested on Will's shoulder. "Well, what do you know?"

Mia rose and pushed back the blankets in the crib. "Lay him on his back," she whispered.

Will settled Billy and Mia reached for the covers, her hand brushing Will's. They both stilled for a second and it seemed as if the temperature in the room rose a degree or two. Then he moved his hand and Mia pulled up the blanket. They both stepped back.

"I should get going," Will said. "Don't imagine I'll be too popular downstairs now."

"I'll walk you to your car," Mia said. "I could use the fresh air. Let me get my coat from my room. It's just next door."

Will waited in the doorway, blinking in disbelief at the memorabilia of the dead war hero. He wandered closer to a photographic portrait. Jared had been a good-looking guy but—and admittedly, he could be biased—there was something shifty about his eyes.

Mia turned from the dresser with a pair of gloves. "Nora did all this. She likes to feel that Jared is with us still."

"You must be suffocating," Will said bluntly.

Mia just shook her head wearily and moved past him into the hall. They went down a second staircase at the other end of the hall that led to the kitchen. Will got his jacket and they set off down the driveway. His mind reeled at this glimpse into the life Mia led here. It must be what she wanted or she wouldn't be staying. But a young, vital woman living in a mausoleum—it wasn't right. And Billy… His hands curled at his sides thinking of the boy's future.

"I met your mom and dad," he said to stop himself thinking about Mia's situation. "They're awfully nice. Couldn't you stay with them?"

"They don't have room, or believe me, I'd be there in a heartbeat." Mia turned left on the sidewalk, following Will's gesture, and flipped up her jacket collar against the wind.

"Well, this is me." Will stopped beside his truck, parked a block away. "I'll give you a ride back to the house."

"No, I could use a few extra minutes on my own," Mia said. "Thanks for coming. And for agreeing to be Billy's godfather. He needs someone like you in his life."

"I can see that," Will said. "I'll do my best by him, I promise." He started to open the door of his truck.

Mia put a hand on his sleeve. "What's the name of your friends' vineyard? I…I might apply after all."

Hallelujah. He pulled a business card from his pocket and handed it to Mia. "Just happened to have this with me."

She smiled up at him and the wind blew a strand of dark hair across her face. He brushed it back and held on to the end, feeling the silky texture. Her mouth looked soft and warm and pliable, her eyes large and luminous. Everything in him wanted to lower his mouth to hers but Nora's warning in the kitchen made him hold back. She was still in love with her late husband. *Don't do it. Don't spoil your friendship.* If he came on too strong he would scare her off and then he'd be sorry.

While he was tormenting himself with doubt, Mia leaned up and kissed him briefly. She drew back, regarded him with grave dark eyes, then kissed him again, her warm lips lingering on his a fraction of a second too long to be considered merely platonic. The taste of her left him craving more.

She backed away, fingertips to her lips. "That didn't happen."

"I'm pretty sure it did." And he wouldn't deny it, not if someone paid him.

"It's not a good idea, though," she said. "You're on the rebound. And I'm…not in the right place."

"I'm not…" He stopped himself from telling her that he wasn't on the rebound, that Katie wasn't an issue. "I'm not in a good place, either." More than anything he didn't want to lose contact with Mia. If she thought he was avoiding romantic entanglements because his breakup was too fresh then she wouldn't feel pressured by being around him. She would feel safe and they could be friends. He touched her cheek. "I'll see you soon."

He got into his truck and started to drive off. Mia began to walk back to the house. He glanced in his rearview mirror just before he turned the corner. Her hair was blowing back in a gust, exposing her neck, and her skirt blew up, revealing long, smooth legs.

It had been quite a day. A laugh from his godson. A kiss from Mia. She might be grieving for Jared but she had a small space in her heart for him, too.

He had no idea when he would see her again but he couldn't wait. And yes, he was an idiot.

Chapter Ten

Two months later…

FROM THE LIVING room of her second-story apartment Mia watched a teenaged couple walk hand in hand down 1st Street in Sweetheart. A moment ago she'd dialed Will's number and now the phone was ringing and her stomach was full of butterflies. She could see the girl's face as she looked up at her boyfriend—excited, giggly, alive. That was exactly how she felt. *Please pick up, Will…*

"Mia," he finally said in his deep voice, slightly out of breath. "Hang on, I'm in the middle of fixing the tire on the tractor." There was a clatter of tools in the background and then he said, "What's up?"

"Guess what?" she said, grinning. She wished they were on Skype and she could see his face but she could picture him, his blond hair dented by his cowboy hat and the knees of his jeans dusty from kneeling on the ground.

"You won the lottery? That's what you sound like." There was amusement in his tone and metal clanking noises, as if he was putting tools away.

"I got the job at your friends' vineyard," she said triumphantly.

"Awesome!" Will said. "Does that mean you're going to live here?"

"I rented an apartment above the Beauty Spot on 1st Street," she said. "It's right across from City Hall."

"I know the salon," Will said. "Emma's sister Zoe owns it."

"There's a little park and a playground half a block away. Laney is on the next street. The apartment is furnished, too." Mia turned to survey the plain but comfortable furniture. "It's not going to make the cover of *House Beautiful* but it'll do just fine until I can save enough money for a deposit on a home of my own."

"Congratulations," Will said. "When do you take possession? Do you need a hand moving?"

"I'm here now. I hired a moving truck in Billings." With the last of her dwindling savings. She'd figured Will would help if she asked but she'd already imposed on him enough. She wanted to spend time with him because she enjoyed his company, not for what he could do for her. "I drove up last week for the job interview and checked out rental accommodation then. Everything's happened so fast, I can hardly believe it."

"Good for you." Approval warmed Will's voice. "When do you start work?"

"Next week. Three days a week and probably more hours

come June when tourist season is in full swing. Stewart and Kristin are so nice, I know I'm going to love working there. I told them about my uncle's vineyard and trattoria in Umbria and now they want to install a wood-fired pizza oven." She paused for breath. "So the reason I'm calling…"

"You don't need a reason," Will said.

But she did. When she kissed him goodbye at the christening she'd felt her whole being surge to life at the touch of his lips. She'd sensed his attraction to her but also his wariness. The smart thing would be to keep her distance. She had a child now. Changing their relationship from friendly to romantic would be just plain dumb. He probably thought so, too. She needed to be very, very certain before she leapt into another relationship. Especially a romance that was doomed to fail because Will was on the rebound.

Yet here she was, knowing she was doomed and contacting him anyway. She didn't know what would happen between them, she only knew she longed to see him.

"I brought home some wine from the vineyard," she went on. "Can I come by and share it with you to celebrate? You've been instrumental in so much of my good fortune coming to fruition."

"Absolutely," Will said. "I'd love to see you and Billy."

"Oh, that's the other thing!" Mia exclaimed. "Laney's new housemate, Shelley, runs a daycare. She took Billy home after it was finished for the day and Laney's looking after him till I can pick him up."

"Come over now if you want," Will said. "I just need to clean up and I'm heading home."

"Perfect. I'll see you soon." Mia hung up and called Laney to check in. "Hey, how did Billy do today?"

"Great," Laney said. "I just gave him a bottle and now he's asleep."

"Poor little guy must be tuckered out." Mia had almost cried this morning leaving him for the first time in someone else's care for an extended period. But Shelley was a lovely person and Laney had known her for years so there was no reason at all to be worried. "I'm on my way to Will's house. I won't be late."

"Stay as long as you want—I don't mind." Laney paused and added slyly, "You could pick Billy up in the morning if you want."

"That won't be necessary," Mia said firmly. "Will and I are just friends."

"Really?" Laney teased. "I saw the way he looked at you at the christening. When you came back inside after walking him to his car you were all flushed. You never did tell me what happened out there. Did he kiss you?"

"It was purely platonic," Mia said, although that was a flat-out lie. She'd tasted desire on his lips and had longed to put her arms around his neck and deepen the kiss. But Laney's teasing acted like a bucketful of cold water on the fire inside her. She had to stop wishing this thing with Will could lead somewhere. They were both on the rebound, in their own ways. Sweetheart was a small town and everyone knew each other's business. It would be embarrassing for Will, especially, to have his love life scrutinized after being dropped by Katie. And if she and Will had an affair and it ended badly, Billy could suffer, too. And that she couldn't bear.

"If you're waiting for permission, I say, go for it," Laney said. "You need to move on."

"It isn't even a year since Jared died," Mia protested. "Will has his own issues to work out. Anyway, I doubt he'd be interested. He's seen my vagina expand to the size of a melon and a baby come out. *So* not sexy."

"I hope you don't intend to trot out that graphic when you're with him," Laney said, laughing. "But I'm encouraged by the fact that you would even say that. It means you've been thinking about sex with him."

"I'm going to ignore that," Mia said primly. "Do you have enough formula?"

She couldn't say the word without feeling a stab of loss. Her milk had dried up after three months, thanks in part to Nora sabotaging her by giving Billy bottles. She'd tried expressing milk but it was too late. Laney thought tension from living at the Richards' house had contributed to the problem and sadly, Mia suspected she was right.

"I bought a big container on sale at the drugstore," Laney said. "Plus bottles and teething rings."

Mia laughed. "You've gone all out."

"I'm excited to be an aunt," Laney said. "Now go and enjoy yourself with that hottie of yours. If I don't hear from you by ten o'clock, I'll assume you're not coming and I'll go to bed."

Mia didn't bother denying again. She said goodbye and carried the wine down to her car parked around the back of the Beauty Spot.

The drive to Will's place was gorgeous, the road lined with rows and rows of cherry trees in full blossom. Spring had come early this year, the warmest April on record, apparently. She wound down the window and breathed in the delicate perfume of the clusters of thick white blossoms. It was like driving through a fragrant snowdrift. So different from the real and very cold snow she'd encountered the last time she'd come this way.

In a clearing stood Will's sprawling single-story house of stone and timber. A welcoming curl of smoke rose from the chimney. The days might be unseasonably warm but temperatures dropped once the sun went behind the mountains.

She parked next to his truck and grabbed the cardboard carry case containing three bottles of wine. After seeing countless photos of the progress of his house she couldn't wait to see it in real life. Face it, she admitted wryly, she couldn't wait to see Will.

The door opened before she could knock.

"Come in." Will stepped back to let her enter a spacious foyer. His hair was damp from the shower and his light blue

T-shirt straining across broad shoulders made his blue eyes pop. Laney was right. He was hot. Tall, too. She'd forgotten how he towered over her.

"Hey," she said, slightly breathless.

"Hey, yourself." Smiling, he pulled her into a hug, enveloping her in warmth and strength.

She could easily have lingered in his embrace but instead she held up the carton containing the wine. "I thought it would be fun to do some blind tasting."

"Cool." He took them from her. "Come in."

The faint lingering smell of fresh paint hit her but it was a clean scent, not overpowering. Walls were finished, tiles were laid underfoot in the foyer and leading to the kitchen. Beyond in the living room, a beautiful hardwood floor gleamed. Sparse furniture, nothing on the walls, no plants. But there was a lot of potential.

"It's a work in progress," he said. "But I'm getting there."

"I love it already." Her gaze met his and bounced away again. Seeing each other at the christening had brought a new awareness to the surface. This shouldn't feel like a date. But it did. A rather formal, stilted first date. Which was ridiculous considering he'd already seen her naked and in the most vulnerable position a woman could ever be in.

She followed him into the kitchen where delicious aromas of chicken, tomato and herbs filled the air. The light, bright room was done in beechwood and black tiles with accents of slate green. "Did you get a designer or did you do this yourself?"

"I picked materials and colors that appealed to me and hoped for the best." He rubbed his hands together, seemingly nervous, too. "I put chicken cacciatore in the slow cooker this morning. I've been trying to eat more healthily now that the house is mostly finished and I have more time. I hope you'll join me for dinner."

"I'd love to," she said matching his polite and formal tone. They both needed to calm the hell down and relax enough to talk to each other normally. Wine would help. She started removing the bottles from the carton. "Have you got six glasses?"

He opened a cupboard and brought down stacks of small water glasses. "Will these do?"

"Perfect. Now turn around and don't look." She poured a taste out of the first bottle and put it back into the carton so the label was hidden. "I've got three reds of different grape varieties. Your mission, should you choose to accept it, is to identify the variety and the year." She was joking but she thought Will would enjoy the challenge. "Okay, ready."

Will took a glass, swirled the wine and held it up to the light. "Bright ruby red. I'd guess it's a young wine."

"Very good." She nodded approvingly.

He sniffed. "Bouquet of pepper and blackberry with overtones of leather and muskrat."

Mia laughed. "Now you're mocking me."

"Oh, am I wrong about the blackberry?" Humor danced

in his eyes.

"Forget the quiz," she said. "Let's just drink."

"Thank goodness. I don't know much about wine," Will said. "But I—"

"Know what I like," she finished. "Taste them all and just tell me which one you prefer. Later we can try them with the chicken to see which is the best match."

Will took a sip and moved the wine around his mouth. "It's smooth and mellow. Stop me if I get too technical."

Mia tasted, too, but decided not to bore him by going on about the flavors and the length of finish. If she was at work she would spit it out and rinse her mouth with water or eat a piece of bread. Instead she swallowed. Enjoyment was the aim tonight and it felt good to be doing something just for fun. "Ready for number two?"

"Hit me." Will set out two clean glasses on the granite counter. "It's nice that Laney's willing to babysit Billy."

"Oh, she's willing. I'm half afraid she won't give him back." Mia poured and they tasted. She schooled herself not to grimace but the wine was too young. This bottle she'd siphoned straight out of the cask and it didn't have a label. She would recommend to Stewart that he let it age another year before bottling.

"Not crazy about that one." Will poured the rest of his down the sink. "Don't tell Stewart I said that."

"It'll be fine in a couple more years," Mia said, pouring hers out, too. "Nothing wrong with your taste buds."

Will leaned against the counter. "So are you a…what is it you call a wine maker?"

"An enologist. No, I'm not qualified but I had a sort of apprenticeship under my uncle in Italy." After she'd returned to Montana she'd planned to go to college and get her degree. Instead she'd met Jared and gotten married. Life had become too full, too chaotic, too taken up with Jared's wants and needs. "I'll continue my studies more formally when Billy's older. But for now…" she shrugged "…I'll do what I can, maybe take an online course."

They sampled the third wine, a five-year-old Syrah, rich and dark with hints of chocolate, pepper and plum.

"Hands down, this is my favorite," Will said.

"I agree. There's no question." Mia poured out more for both of them. "Cheers."

Will clinked. "It's hard juggling your own life when you're a single mom with a baby. My mother was on her own until I was six years old. She had help from an aunt but there was an emotional toll."

"Billy is worth any hardship and I'm sure your mom thought the same about you." After a pause Mia asked, "So, Robert isn't your father?"

"He is," Will said. "He and Mom split up for a while before getting back together again."

"And in the interval your half brother Alex came along," Mia guessed, her forehead wrinkled.

"It's complicated. I'll tell you sometime. But for now,

come, I'll give you the tour." He led the way out of the kitchen and around the corner to a short hall. "On the left is the laundry room, then the bathroom…"

"Beautiful marble," Mia exclaimed, seeing the richly veined ivory stone lining the floor and shower stall. "In Carrara, Italy, where that marble comes from, they pave the streets with it."

"Seriously?" Will said. "I'd like to see that."

"Maybe someday you will." Mia entertained a brief fantasy of the two of them, and Billy of course, traveling through Italy. She would love to show him the country of her ancestors. The land of *amore*.

Will gestured as he walked on. "Bedroom two, linen closet, bedroom three. Not much to see so far. All I've done is paint." He stopped at the end of the hall. "The master bedroom needs more furniture and decoration. I can sleep here but that's about it."

Mia stepped inside the large room, lined on one side with mirrored closets facing a king-size bed covered in a sage green comforter. A desk lamp sat atop an upturned crate used as a makeshift nightstand. The afternoon sun streaming through western-facing windows made the walls glow butter yellow and brought a warm gleam to the curved wooden headboard.

"Nice bed," she said since there was nothing else to comment on, then murmured, "You could do more here than sleep." Silence. Had she really said that? Turning slowly, her mouth dry, she saw his gaze fixed on her. The look in his eyes made her unable to catch her breath. "Will?"

"I'm so very tired of fighting this." He set his glass down on the chest and with one step, took her face in his hands. His long fingers speared through her hair as he lowered his mouth to hers. The pads of his fingers and palms were callused but his hands gentle as he explored and tasted her. After only a moment's hesitation, her arms went around his neck, pulling him closer, feeling the physical reality of him. The softness of his cotton shirt, the hardness of the muscle and bone beneath. Her resolve to keep things platonic was dissolving at the first hurdle. What was wrong with her?

She pushed him away. "I can't—"

He released her immediately, head bowed, hands on hips. "Sorry. I can't believe I'm hitting on a grieving widow."

"Will, I like you so much," she said. "You're a great guy and so attractive—"

His expression turned agonized and he held up a hand to fend off her words. "Okay, I know where this is going—"

"No, I mean it." She reached for him, sliding her hands up his tanned forearms dusted with blond hair to his biceps, feeling the muscles and bones. So strong. "When I'm around you, I'm…helpless to resist."

He stilled and then slid the back of his hand over her cheek to trace the curve of her throat. His eyes followed the movement and she could feel the touch of his gaze as much as his fingers. "Are you sure you want to resist me?"

JOAN KILBY

"No…" She leaned closer and he took her in his arms to kiss her hungrily. Her insides turned hot and liquid. "Wait." Panting, she pushed him away again with a moan. The words came out in a rush, all the reasons this wasn't going to work. "I have a tiny baby. I need to focus on building my life for him. I'm too impulsive. I don't want to ever again get so caught up in desire that my brain takes a holiday."

"I'm not Jared." Will's words grated out.

"No, you're nothing like him," Mia said. "But you're on the rebound. You're vulnerable. I'm not ready for a serious relationship. I would hate to hurt you."

Huffing out a laugh, he reached for her hand, circled a thumb around her palm. "I'm not a delicate flower."

His thumb sent shivers along her nerve endings. Her eyes flickered shut, her determination wavering. She couldn't think. "We…can't. Please."

Reluctantly, he let Mia's hand go. "I understand. You're still grieving for your husband."

She hesitated. Jared wasn't the issue but it would be easier if Will thought so. "You were with Katie for ten years. Neither of us is ready to start anything serious."

Will frowned, seemed about to say something, then stopped and just nodded.

Mia bit her lip. Wasn't he going to try to change her mind? No sooner had he agreed with her than she wanted to convince him otherwise. Oh, she was crazy bad, she was—

An alternate scenario popped into in her head. They

didn't have to be serious. No one was talking marriage or even long term. They could start something purely for fun. A no-strings affair.

Pressing her fingers to her temples, she crossed to the window and laid her hot forehead to the cold glass, frightened of herself. It was happening again. She was leaping impulsively into a relationship only this time she could clearly see the dangers. There was too much at stake. One of them, or even both, would get hurt. Billy could get hurt. He already got excited when he saw Will. If things went wrong, and Will didn't come around anymore… No, it was too risky.

In the window's reflection she could see Will waiting, watching her, his body taut, hands lightly clenched, long thigh muscles outlined against the fabric of his jeans. Was what she was thinking so wrong? He was hot. And she was a normal, red-blooded woman who'd been without a man's touch for too long. She'd barely noticed the lack until Will had come along but once he had, the craving for a return to normal life had reared up. What was more life-affirming than sex?

"Mia?" Will came up behind her and put his hands on her shoulders and massaged them. "Are you okay?"

Turning, she rested a hand on his chest, felt his heart beating fast and strong beneath the firm muscle and warm skin. Looking into his eyes she got lost in the heat mingled with compassion and kindness. She felt safe with this man.

Safe to let go and feel again. When he'd pulled her in from the storm on Christmas Eve something had been set in motion that was finally coming to fruition. Her emotions might be a tangled mess but right now, right here, making love with him felt not only inevitable, but right and true.

"No one would have to know," she whispered. "If we both understand that it's not serious. It's just no-strings sex with a trusted friend. We could have fun. We could be each other's rebound fling. When the time comes, we say goodbye with no hard feelings and move on."

His hands stilled on her shoulders. "Friends with benefits?" he repeated as though trying the concept on for size.

"Think about it," she said, throwing caution to the wind as she warmed to the idea. "We're attracted to each other. And we're both sex starved, right? I am at least." Will nodded wryly, acknowledging he was in the same position. "If we weren't at the mercy of our hormones, we'd be better placed to eventually make rational decisions about a future partner."

"That almost makes sense," Will said, shaking his head. "But why the secrecy? That doesn't sit right with me."

Because if no one knew they were a couple, she could pretend it wasn't real and the humiliation would be less when Will eventually found someone else. "My husband hasn't been dead a year. It's not seemly."

"We're not living in the olden days," Will said. "There's no rule that says you have to mourn for a whole year."

"My in-laws would think a year isn't nearly long enough," Mia replied. "Besides, do you want everyone to be watching how we're getting along and have expectations of where this might lead?"

"God, no." Will put a hand to his forehead. "Mom wants so much for me to be happy that she'll have me engaged to the first woman I go out with. And she likes you a lot. The whole family does."

"I like them, too, but it's a lot of pressure," Mia said. "We don't need that."

"Damn right." Will gave her a rueful smile then his smile faded. "What if, despite keeping it light and easy, one of us falls in love?"

"It won't happen because we're prepared." Mia stepped closer and put her arms around his waist. She could feel his warm breath on her neck, his body heating her. "Love only blindsides you when you're not expecting it. We'd be going into this with our eyes open."

Will ran his hands down her back. He nuzzled her neck, kissing behind her ear. "You're very persuasive. I keep thinking there's got to be a catch."

"There's only one thing I worry about," she said. "That if anything goes wrong, it'll adversely affect Billy."

"I'm committed to Billy," Will said firmly. "And to you, as a friend. Nothing will ever change that."

The last of her reservations evaporated. "In that case, what have we got to lose?"

Chapter Eleven

SEX FOR FUN, no strings. Will didn't have a problem with that but the secrecy made him uneasy. It felt clandestine even though they weren't cheating on anyone.

On the other hand, fighting his desire for Mia, pretending his feelings were purely platonic, was starting to feel dishonest. He was sick of second-guessing his feelings, of weighing every decision and every emotional reaction. Holding her, kissing her, telling her how much he wanted her—that felt true and right.

He smiled down at Mia. "You have a habit of surprising the hell out of me."

"I surprise myself sometimes," Mia said with a twist to her mouth. "I didn't come here planning to do this. Quite the opposite, in fact. There are so many reasons it's not a great idea—"

"We've been over that so let's not go there again. I can think of one reason a secret affair is a terrific idea." Sliding his hands down to her hips, he nipped at her luscious mouth, licking along the seam, coaxing her to open again. He tasted her sweetness, savoring the warmth and wetness, and his body tightened. He slid his hands under her top in search of bare skin, soft as silk and warm to his touch.

Mia tensed fractionally. Her hands stilled on his shoulders and her kiss felt strained. For a woman who had been eager only a moment ago, she seemed strangely reluctant now that he'd agreed to her scheme.

He tilted her chin to look into her eyes. "You're not with me. Is this is about Jared?"

"No. Sorry, I thought I was ready for this. I was hoping it wouldn't be a problem." Eyes anxious, her pretty mouth twisted. "I gave birth only four months ago."

"Are you still sore? We can take it slow." He pressed a kiss to her temple and behind her ear. "I don't want to hurt you."

"No, everything's back to normal, more or less. But I'm not…the same."

He studied her face for clues and was baffled. "I'm not getting it. Help me out."

"My body has changed. I've got stretch marks." Color bloomed in her cheeks. "God knows what I'm like inside."

As if he cared. "You're beautiful inside," he said deliberately misunderstanding her but sincerely meaning it. "In every sense of the word. Beautiful inside and out."

Slowly, giving her time to stop him if she wanted to, he pulled her sweater over her head. Her full breasts, firmly encased in satin cups, jiggled. The sight made his groin tighten, his hardening cock pushing at his jeans. Sliding his hands down over her waist he undid the top button of her pants and eased down the zipper to run his fingers over her slightly rounded belly. Her skin was pale and smooth.

"Your body looks and feels amazing." He raised his eyebrows, asking permission to continue. She nodded and he felt her relax and melt beneath his hands, his mouth. So hot, so sexy. So real. Dropping to his knees he kissed her stomach, licking along the faint pink lines that angled toward the apex of her thighs. "I like them. They're arrows pointing me in the right direction."

She gave a husky chuckle and speared her fingers through his hair, pulling him closer. Will gave himself over to a thorough exploration of her hips and belly. Women were way too hard on themselves. There was absolutely nothing wrong with Mia's body. Soft and curving here, firm and resilient there. If anything, knowing she'd given birth made her seem more womanly. His fingers tightened over her round butt cheeks as his tongue slipped through the line of soft curls and dipped into the inner folds, slippery as silk, hot and moist. Her musky perfume was as heady as any wine and he was intoxicated with the sheer glory of her. A low growl came from his throat, primeval and animal.

"Oh my," Mia moaned. She pulled him up, seeking his mouth with hers. Her tongue was hot and exciting, thrusting against his. With his splayed hand squeezing her butt, another molding her breast, he could feel the pounding of her heart as a counterpoint to the thrum of his own blood.

He'd wanted her for months, the need for her growing every time he saw her or heard her voice. Repressing his desires hadn't made them go away, it had put them in a pressure cooker that was now ready to explode. Will mashed kisses onto her cheeks, her eyes, her chin. His hands roved everywhere, wanting to touch all of her at once.

Mia was just as eager, tugging his shirt free. Before she could undo all his buttons she abandoned the task and fumbled with his belt, easing the supple leather out of the brass buckle. His erection made it hard for her to slide his zipper down.

"Get your clothes off cowboy," she said, laughing with frustration.

"I'm not a cowboy. I'm an orchardist." He ripped his shirt off and flung it aside. Then got busy with the clasp of her bra as he backed her toward the bed.

"So literal." She stroked her hands down his chest and belly, pushing his jeans down over his hips. "So sexy. Long and lean and hard."

Freed of her bra, her breasts jutted, the dusky nipples standing proudly, just begging to be sucked. Happy to oblige he gave them his full attention—sucking and licking, nipping lightly. Her legs hit the mattress and they went down in a tumble.

He grabbed a condom from the shoebox of bedside stuff on top of the crate then dragged her jeans down to her knees and flipped her over, tugging her panties down, too, to nip her butt cheek.

"Did you just bite me?" Throaty amusement sounded in her voice. Her head was turned to the side, her mass of hair over her face, obscuring her vision.

"Sorry, did it hurt?" He'd meant it to just sting.

"Only in a good way." She edged her hand beneath her, between her legs. "Oh God. I'm going to come lying face down with my pants halfway down my legs. This is so not dignified."

"You never said anything about us having to be dignified." And wasn't that liberating? Katie always had to have the setting and ambience just so—lighting, mood music, not too early in the evening, or too late. How had he never figured out from that they'd lost the spark?

Then the sight and feel of Mia, laughing and struggling, drove that thought and all others from his head. He held her wrists and pinioned her legs, using just enough strength to make it difficult for her to move but not enough to make her feel unsafe while he sheathed himself and then nudged his cock between her thighs, probing for her entrance. She was stronger than she looked, and feisty. She squirmed until she'd turned herself over and lay beneath him, diagonally across the bed. The sunset turned her cheeks golden and sent fiery sparks into her hair. He loomed over her, his hard, straining cock reaching for her. Her bare breasts heaved as she panted, her back arched above the mattress.

She pushed her mass of dark hair off her face. "I want you inside me. Now."

"Yes, ma'am." He shucked off his jeans and lowered his naked body onto hers.

She moaned and held him, wrapping arms and legs around him. He thrust into her and moved in a steady rhythm that felt incredibly good. She matched him thrust for thrust, her hips working steadily, rhythmically. Perspiration formed on his forehead, his arms and his chest. She stroked down to cup his taut butt that flexed and pushed. He watched her face, admiring how she wallowed in pleasure, giving herself over to the sensuality of the act, touching and tasting and savoring.

Her sudden gasp and tightened grip signaled her mood had shifted to greater urgency. Taut muscles became rock hard, tendons strained, flesh pounded. Suddenly her eyes rolled back and she came with all the intensity of an imploding star. He was caught unawares, dragged from his own climax by attention to her needs. She gripped him, riding wave after wave, then collapsed with a cry, her eyelids fluttering.

Will's body thrummed with unrelieved tension. He lay on his side and pulled her into his arms, holding her and stroking her hair back from her damp face. He was still inside her, a leg wrapped around her hip, holding her in place. Hanging on to his control, trying to be patient.

She stirred and blinked. "Did you come?"

He traced a fingertip down her neck. "Doesn't matter."

"Oh, yes it does." Pushing him off her, she straddled him. Placing her hands on his shoulders she sat up on him and started to move, squeezing herself around his swollen cock. "How does this feel?"

"Good." Massive understatement. Delaying his climax had amped up the tension, increased the pleasure. His eyes started to glaze over. He took her butt in his hands and moved her in a different rhythm, which she tried to match but couldn't quite. The resulting slight discordance only increased the urgency. Every muscle of his body, every fiber of hers, strained taut and tense. The cords on his neck stood out and beads of perspiration appeared on his forehead. *Now...* He groaned and thrust hard.

Mia cried suddenly as another orgasm took her, triggering his own release. Together they rode the aftershocks, their twined bodies tight and shuddering. With a final grind of her hips to wring out the last bit of pleasure she collapsed on top of him, spent.

Will held her, feeling damp warm skin. Listened to her breathing next to his ear. Had sex ever been this good before? He couldn't remember an occasion. He had to stop comparing. It wasn't fair. But this... Eyes closed, he smiled. Oh, man, this felt like a first.

After what seemed like ages, he opened his eyes. Shadows of trees moved against the ocher walls in the dying sun. There was stillness and a timeless quality to the light. They could have been in Paris or Rome or Seville. He'd never been to those places, mind you. He might go someday but if not, it didn't matter. Everything he needed was right here at home. When the gold had faded to silver Mia lifted her head. Her cooling perspiration raised goose bumps down her slender arms.

"Get under the covers," he said and shifted so she could crawl into the bed. He got in beside her and pulled her into the crook of his arm so her head rested on his shoulder. "Okay?"

"Awesome," she said. "Guess I haven't forgotten how to do it after all."

"It's like riding a bike." His soft chuckle tickled her ear as he stroked a hand down her arm. "You're one hot mamma."

As if he'd pressed a trigger, she shot up in bed and glanced at the bedside clock. Nearly seven p.m. "I should go pick up Billy or Laney's going to think we're doing exactly what we're doing."

"It's still early," he said. "You haven't had dinner yet. Text her and see how Billy is, set your mind at rest."

"Okay, you're right." She got out of bed and grabbed his shirt to put on for the trek to the kitchen to find her phone.

Will got up, too, pulled on his boxers and followed her out to check the chicken. He took off the lid and released a waft of aromatic steam. Poking it with a fork, the meat fell softly off the bone. Perfect. He poured two fresh glasses from the third bottle of wine.

Mia received an immediate reply from Laney. "She says Billy's fine. He's awake but happy."

"He's in good hands. If there's any problem you can be at Laney's in five minutes." Will handed her the glass of wine. "Relax and enjoy some adult time."

"Much as I adore my baby, I do crave adult time." Flushed from lovemaking, with his shirt buttoned up wrong and her bare thighs, she looked incredibly beautiful and sexy. She raised her glass. "To a secret, no-strings fling."

An unexpected shaft of annoyance over the secrecy aspect streaked through his consciousness. He blinked in surprise at the vehemence of his feeling. Then he pushed it away and clinked glasses. It was worth anything to have this time with Mia. "No strings."

They took the wine and chicken and ate on deck chairs in the living room. The gas fireplace brought a cozy atmosphere to the sparsely furnished room.

"This food is amazing," Mia said, devouring her chicken.

Will reached for the bottle of wine to top her up but Mia put her hand over her glass. "No more for me."

"Tell Laney you've been drinking and you're going to stay over," Will suggested.

"No. I'm going to pick up Billy after dinner and go home. Otherwise, she won't believe nothing's going on between us." Mia stabbed at a piece of chicken. "You know, if we spend time together people are going to notice."

He felt himself tense. "Would that be so bad?"

Her raised eyebrows reminded him of what they'd talked about before hitting the sheets. She was right. The last thing he wanted was people asking him about Mia. Were they serious? How did he feel about being with a single mom? Was he really over Katie? He let his breath go, forcing himself to relax.

"We need a cover story," Mia said, sopping up sauce with a piece of crusty bread.

"You could help me decorate my house?" Will suggested.

"Because I'm so good at that." She snorted with laughter. "Laney won't believe that."

"But she might believe you would help me because you're a nice person."

"We're overthinking this," Mia said. "Friends do stuff together. You have a brand-new house. I could use some home wares myself. It makes sense if we go shopping together. Laney told me about a place called The Flathead Shed, a collection of antique and vintage shops on Route 35."

"My mother goes there all the time." Will said. "How about this Saturday?" Three days away. Could he wait?

"It's a date." Mia winked. "Or, you know, not."

Chapter Twelve

THE NEXT DAY, Thursday, Mia put Billy in his stroller and walked over to Main Street and along to the Cherry Pit. She hadn't expected to see Will today but just as she arrived at the diner, his truck pulled in across the street and parked in front of Starr Realty.

She waited on the sidewalk while he stepped out of the vehicle, admiring his athletic grace and the breadth of his shoulders. Seeing her, he stopped dead, and then his mouth kicked up in a smile. Mia's heart beat double time and she waved, biting her cheek to stop from grinning like a loon. Will lifted a hand and nonchalantly turned to enter his father's office. Smiling, Mia continued into the diner, dragging the stroller in backward over the sill.

"Morning, Skye," she called to the waitress as she passed the counter, heading for what was fast becoming her regular table at the back. "Latte and a blueberry muffin, please."

"Coming right up." Skye moved over to the coffee machine.

Mia removed Billy's hat and mittens and undid the zip

on his jacket. She handed him teething ring to chew and then checked her phone to see if there was a message from Will.

CU in 5.

Mia smiled to herself. There was nothing illicit about what they were doing but for her the secret nature of their affair added to the excitement. And it was freeing. No one was questioning her on the wisdom of hooking up with Billy's godfather, or wondering how she felt being with a new man, the first since Jared. Nor were Will's family or friends quietly weighing her up, seeing how she stacked up compared to Katie, or judging whether Will was even over Katie yet and could actually care about Mia. It was all about her and Will and the pleasure they felt in each other's company.

Will came into the diner a few minutes later. He ordered a coffee to go then casually strolled over. "Coffee break?"

"Yes. Do you want to join me?" she said, pushing out a chair next to Billy's buggy.

"I have to get back to the orchard but I can sit while I wait for my coffee." His eyes said everything that his words didn't—pleasure at seeing her, remembrance of their evening together, anticipation of Saturday. "How are you?"

"Good." She felt her cheeks heat and kept her gaze lowered, suddenly aware how hard it was to hide infatuation.

Billy knew nothing of pretense. Delighted at seeing Will,

and not afraid to show it, he gurgled and waved his arms, slapping the jingle bells on the side of his stroller.

"Hey, buddy." Will captured Billy's foot and pretended to bite it, eliciting more baby chuckles. Beneath the table, Will's boot slid next to Mia's shoe, their calves touching.

"What brings you to town?" Mia asked, pressing her leg into his. "Did you drop by to see your father?"

His hand, hidden by the checked tablecloth, found her knee and he lightly stroked the inside of her thigh. "I delivered some papers for Dad's signature. What are you up to?"

"Coffee, then shopping. There's a wonderful produce market two doors down." She leaned back so Skye could set down her coffee and muffin. When the waitress moved away Mia said with a meaningful glance, "I plan to stay in this afternoon and make cookies."

"I like cookies," he said with a lazy smile. "What kind?"

She licked foam off her spoon very slowly. "Ginger-snaps."

"My favorite."

"Drop by for some later if you like."

"I'll see what I can do." He gave her a salute in farewell.

He joked with Skye as he picked up his coffee then went out without a backward glance. It was only when he was outside that he looked back through the window and smiled a slow smile directly at her. Mia's pulse quickened. This afternoon couldn't come fast enough.

Her apartment smelled like ginger and cinnamon when Will knocked several hours later. Mia opened the door in her apron, her hair tied back in a ribbon. This was the first time Will had been to her place and she felt flustered when he filled her doorway. "Come in."

He held out a plant pot from which emerged a single long thick stalk topped by a large tumescent bud, the green sepals ready to burst open on red petals. "Housewarming gift."

"Is that phallic or what?" She laughed. "What on earth is it?"

"An amaryllis." Will kicked the door closed and kissed her, hard and sweet. "It's a bulb. Keep it and it'll bloom again next year."

Billy shrieked at Will's arrival and waved his arms and legs, making his bouncer rock on the hardwood floor.

The oven timer beeped. Mia hurried back to the kitchen and pulled out a tray of ginger snaps. Will picked Billy out of the bouncer and lifted him high into the air. Billy giggled and wriggled, stretching out his arms to Will.

Mia lifted cookies off the pan onto a cooling rack. "He should be ready for his nap soon."

"No rush." Will tucked Billy in the crook of his arm and chatted to him about a problem he was having with the cherry processor. Although the words were technical and far beyond Billy's understanding, Will's tone was warm and caring, punctuated by tickles. Billy loved it.

Watching her lover and her son interact gave Mia a sharp pang. The other night, when it was just the two of them, she'd been able to push aside her concerns about Billy. But now, seeing how the child adored Will, her doubts came back. Her own feelings were so complicated she could hardly decipher them. If only Will wasn't coming out of a long-term relationship. If only she was in a better place in her life. If only what she and Will had didn't feel so temporary. Despite her grand words about not being blindsided, she was falling for him. He never spoke about Katie and she didn't know if that was a good thing or a bad thing. Was he getting over his ex, or was he so deeply hurt that he was repressing his emotions?

Will placed Billy on his tummy on a sheepskin rug and sat cross-legged next to him. He pulled a yellow and brown stuffed giraffe from his jacket pocket and pretended to be surprised. "Whoa, where did that come from?" Billy grabbed at the soft toy and rolled over, shaking it and blowing bubbles. To Mia, Will said, "He's really growing fast."

"He just started rolling over yesterday." Mia put another pan in the oven and brought over a plate of warm ginger-snaps. She sat on the floor and offered them to Will.

He bit into a soft, moist cookie and his eyes widened in surprise. The rest of the cookie disappeared in two bites. "Delicious."

She leaned over and kissed him. "You taste like sugar and spice and everything nice."

"That's my line," he protested. "Speaking of sugar…" He wrapped a hand around the back of her neck to hold her steady and licked at the corner of her mouth. "You had a bit there."

"Mmm." She got on all fours and kissed him back, opening to allow his tongue to sweep through her mouth. This wasn't love, she reminded herself. It was sex. Fabulous sex. As long as she didn't get too close, or let him see how she felt, she could enjoy their time together for what it was, not what she wished it would be.

Will started to pull her onto his lap. "Let's get comfortable."

"Hold that thought." She glanced at Billy and saw that his eyelids were starting to flutter and close. "I'm going to put this little guy to bed."

She carried him to his bedroom and laid him in his cot. He stirred at being placed down and she patted him until he dropped off again. When she got back to the kitchen the timer was beeping and Will was taking the last pan of cookies out of the oven.

"So." She put her arms around him from behind. "Let me show you the rest of the place."

She took his hand and led him to her room, which she'd made ready with scented candles on the dresser and condoms handy in the bedside table drawer. The curtains were closed against the afternoon sun but the room was filled with a soft light. They undressed each other slowly and took their time exploring each other's bodies. The radio in the living room played soft music. Traffic sounds filtered in from the street. Will kissed her breasts, the inside of her upper arm, the backs of her knees, inside her thighs.

She tracked the lines of his abs and the hard muscles of his biceps and shoulders. It was different than last time but no less pleasurable. Few words were uttered; their language was the language of touch and locked gazes. Kisses and sighs. They made love with languorous ease, building pleasure upon pleasure until her skin tingled and her core ached and her breath came in short pants.

"Now," she said as Will loomed over her.

"A little more." His taut muscles glistened as he moved in her with long slow thrusts.

"Please," Mia begged.

"Look at me." His eyes were azure and fathomless, like the wide Montana sky.

She squeezed her thighs together, bringing herself to the crest of a wave. "Now."

They climaxed together in a long swooning clench that went on and on until it finally faded, leaving her limp and satiated. Will rolled to one side and pulled her into his arms, their legs still entwined, and stroked her hair. Gradually her heart rate slowed and her skin cooled. She breathed in his scent, his clean warm skin musky with lovemaking, and longed to freeze this moment in time.

Exactly the kind of thought she couldn't allow herself.

There was no point wishing for the impossible.

Easing out of his arms, she sat up and swung her legs over the side of the bed. It was important to keep this only about sex. No lying in each other's arms afterward, no pillow talk or sharing hopes and dreams. Laughter was good but not heartfelt chats. She couldn't do all that and walk away when the time came.

"Are you getting up?" Will said.

"Just felt like sitting."

He moved across the bed and put his arm around her to nuzzle her neck. "Garret's birthday is this weekend. My parents are having a few people over. Would you like to come?"

She would love to come. But why did he ask when he knew what the answer would be? "I thought we weren't going public."

"It would be mainly family."

"They're the ones with the expectations, remember?" Mia hid her regret in a teasing tone. She hated to disappoint him, and herself. Maybe she should have played the long game, let him have other women, get over Katie. But patience had never been her strength. And her feelings were never frivolous.

Obviously troubled, Will dragged a hand through his bed-messed hair. "I don't like sneaking around. Someone's going to find out sooner or later and then we'll feel stupid because there's no reason."

JOAN KILBY

"Have you seen Katie lately?" Mia said.

"What? No." He frowned. "Why do you ask?"

"You never talk about her." Mia ran a thumbnail along the piping at the edge of the quilt cover. "How are you feeling? Are you still angry? Hurt?"

"I don't want to talk about Katie," he said. "I'm here, aren't I? I want to focus on you."

"You can't suppress your feelings forever." She smoothed away the frown lines on his forehead. "Not that I mind being anesthetic for your pain."

He opened his mouth to say something then closed it again. Shrugged and found a smile. "Whatever you say, Doc." His hand cupped her breast and he stroked her with his thumb. "How about a heavy dose of TLC, stat?"

She kissed him, relieved and at the same time, perversely disappointed that he wasn't pushing the issue of going public. Did that mean this was a game to him? "Are we still going shopping on Saturday?"

Will's eyes narrowed. "How is that okay and my brother's party isn't? Just curious."

In the other room, Billy started to make soft babbling sounds to himself in his crib. Even though he could lie there happily for ten or twenty minutes, Mia reached for her clothes.

"Shopping is more impersonal," she said. "You're showing me around, helping out a newcomer to the area. It's not necessarily a date."

170

A shadow of the coming future plunged her heart into sadness. There would be a time when Will would tire of having a girlfriend he couldn't acknowledge openly. When he would be over the rebound and ready for commitment again.

When he would go looking for the real thing.

Timing counted for a lot in relationships and sadly, when it came to her and Will, no matter how awesome the sex and how fun it was to be with him, their lives were out of sync.

"DO PEOPLE REALLY buy this old stuff?" Will gestured to a reproduction Louis IV chair with spindly legs and a faded silk cushion. He preferred clean modern lines and so far he hadn't seen anything he thought would suit his house. The Flathead Shed, a huge antique and vintage consignment complex in an old fruit packing shed, contained a vast array of items, from nineteenth-century clocks to Venetian glass to handmade lace tablecloths. Most of what they were trawling through looked like junk to him but Mia seemed to love this stuff, flitting from shop to shop within the complex, exclaiming over each new find.

"There are some treasures in here," Mia said, retrieving Billy's toy giraffe, which he kept throwing over the side of the buggy. She ran a hand over the scalloped back of a 1920s couch with rolled arms and worn brown upholstery. "If you recovered that it would look good as new."

Will walked around the couch, considering. It was long enough for him to lie full length on and the style reminded him of the love seat in the cottage from his grandparents' era. He'd thought he wanted modern but maybe he ought to keep an open mind. "It would look great in the living room," he conceded.

She sat down and leaned back. "It's comfy, too."

Will dropped down next to her and nuzzled her neck, making her squirm with pleasure. "Who knows what we could get up to on here."

Mia wriggled away and stood, glancing around to see if anyone was looking. "Not here."

Will's mouth compressed. He didn't give a damn who saw and he was starting to regret agreeing to keep their relationship secret. At first it had seemed like a good idea but now it felt restrictive. Okay, making out on a couch in a store might not be a very adult thing to do but it bothered him that she couldn't come to Garret's birthday, or even be seen holding hands on the streets of Sweetheart. He didn't find the secrecy fun or titillating. It made what they did together feel somehow…shameful.

She gave him a worried glance when he continued to sit there grimly and he sighed. Her keeping him at arm's length for a decent mourning period was Mia's way of honoring her late husband and he needed to respect that. But how long would he have to wait? He was losing hope that their no-strings affair would ever turn into something more meaningful.

"Do you folks need help?" A middle-aged woman with shoulder-length brown hair greeted them with a friendly smile. Her name tag read, Carmen.

"How much is this couch?" Will asked, rising. "I didn't see a price tag."

"It just came in yesterday from an estate sale," Carmen said. "It's circa 1926 and solid as anything. You don't get furniture like this these days." She named a price that made Will's eyebrows rise.

"I don't know," Will said. "That's a lot of money and I'd still have to pay to recover it." He started to move away.

"Wait," Carmen said. "You're such a cute family I might be able to do a better price." She took off ten percent and Will accepted even as he wondered how Mia was reacting to Carmen's comment about them being a family.

Billy threw his giraffe overboard again. Carmen, smiling indulgently, bent to pick up the stuffed toy and handed it back to Billy who accepted it gravely. "There you go, cutie pie." She glanced at Will and back to the baby. "He's the spitting image of his daddy."

Will's gaze shot to Mia. Her face was frozen. He'd been mistaken for Billy's father at the hospital but then she'd barely noticed in the exhausted aftermath of the birth. Well-meaning people like Carmen weren't to know that Billy no longer had a father but it must be awful for Mia to get these constant reminders that she'd lost her partner and the future they'd planned together. He wished he could hug away her sadness but in light of what had just happened on the couch, he didn't dare.

"I'm not—" he began apologetically.

"He looks like himself," Mia said evenly, cutting off his explanation.

Carmen looked uncertainly from Will to Mia to Billy. "Well, yes, now that you mention it, I believe you're right. He's still a cutie pie."

"Thanks for your help," Will said, changing the subject. "Where do I pay?"

"This way," Carmen said and started to lead him through a maze of furniture to a desk in a far corner.

"I'll be over there," Mia said, pointing to a display of linen in an adjoining room.

At the desk, Will handed over his credit card and arranged to have the couch delivered. When he got back to Mia she was examining an elaborately crocheted tablecloth. "You okay?"

"Fine." Her blank expression made it impossible to know what she was thinking.

Will picked up a doily he had zero interest in. "A bit awkward when she thought I was Billy's dad."

"No big deal," Mia said. "We don't owe anyone explanations." She pushed Billy down a side aisle toward a display of kitchen gadgets from another century.

"I would have said I was the godfather but it sounds so Mafia," Will said in a lame attempt at humor.

Mia managed a faint smile. "Yes, with your blond hair and blue eyes you're a ringer for Don Corleone."

Will picked up a brass corkscrew and turned it over without really seeing it. Carmen's mistake wasn't important but the wider implications of what he and Mia were doing could be. If complete strangers thought he was Daddy what must Billy think? Okay, the baby was too young to think in those terms but their bond was definitely growing. Already Billy followed him with his gaze and smiled every time he saw Will. And Will loved that. But were he and Mia being fair to the child? How long could they go on like this?

Sooner or later Mia would meet a man she wanted to have a real relationship with and Will would have to take a step back. He would hate for Billy to feel like he'd been abandoned or rejected. He still recalled how hurt and confused he'd been as a child when his dad had divided his time between Sweetheart and his other family in Canada. Every time his dad went away for an extended period he'd felt like he'd been kicked in the guts. To think Billy might feel even a fraction as bad was intolerable.

Will chucked the corkscrew back in the box with the rest of the jumble. Mia made love enthusiastically, even with abandon. But whereas his feelings were growing, whenever they started to get close emotionally, she pulled away. She made love with her body, but not with her heart. That was locked up tight, the possession of another man.

Still he wanted her. What kind of fool did that make him?

He looked around for her and spotted her going through a bin of colorful cushions. Catching up, he asked, "Are these for you?"

"I'll get some but these shot orange silk ones would go beautifully on your bed, don't you think?"

He wouldn't have picked it but now that she suggested it, he could see she was right. "You undersold yourself. You've got good taste. I think you like decorating."

"I can't do much with a rental but I must admit it's fun to think about your place. It's a blank slate."

"Be my guest."

She gave him a small, pained smile. "It's your house. You should make the decisions."

They walked on, moving out of linens and into mirrors, lamps and glassware. Mia remained quiet. Something was bothering her and Will didn't know how to draw her out. "Did you and Jared have a house together?" he asked finally. "What happened to that?"

"After he died, I couldn't keep up the payments."

"Oh." Will had assumed she'd moved to get away from painful memories. "Didn't he have life, or income, insurance? I would have thought that coming from such a wealthy family he would be up on those things. Especially since he was going off to war and leaving a wife behind."

"He had life insurance. He also had a lot of debt. Can we

talk about something else?" Mia checked the price tag on a Tiffany-style lamp and moved on.

"This is nice." Will studied the lamp's delicate painted glass shade and heavy brass base. A possible reason for Mia's somber mood struck him suddenly. The anniversary of Jared's death must be coming up. Maybe it was insensitive to probe but he couldn't help himself. "Was Jared killed around this time last year?"

She turned over a box of glass coasters and didn't respond. It wasn't until she sniffed and used the hem of her sleeve to blot her eyes that he realized she was crying. Not caring who might be watching, Will put his arms around her and drew her close. "Sorry, I shouldn't have mentioned it."

"Saturday a week from today." Her voice wavered. "Nora wants me to go to Billings and attend a special mass for him."

He stroked her hair, so soft and silky. "Are you going?"

"I don't want to." She looked up at him, her eyes huge and dark. "Does that make me a bad person?"

"Absolutely not." Will kissed her tear-stained cheek. "You can remember him in your own way. You don't need a fancy ceremony."

"I don't want to be reminded publicly of my loss, to cry in front of strangers, and have them pity me." Billy began to fuss and she eased out of Will's arms to pick him up and rock him back and forth, her cheek resting on his downy head. "Poor Billy. My poor baby boy."

"You shouldn't be alone on that day," Will said. "We'll

do something together."

"I'll be bad company." Mia edged out of his embrace and put Billy back in the stroller. "You are going to want to stay as far from me as you can get on the day."

"Not going to happen," Will said. "I'll figure something out. We'll get you through this together."

She straightened and wiped her eyes. "No strings, no attachment, remember?"

"I would do the same for any friend."

She didn't have a rebuttal for that. "Well, in that case, okay. Thank you."

"Now that's settled…" He glanced around. "We've gotten off track, or at least I have. I should look for a dining table now. Then I'll worry about cushions and lamps."

"See, that's sensible," Mia said, smiling. "That's why I like you so much."

"You like me because I'm sensible?" he said, grinning. "I didn't know whether to be flattered or sign up for sword-swallowing lessons."

Mia laughed and her eyes sparkled. All was well again.

"I'm taking this, though." He grabbed the Tiffany lamp and put it in the cart.

"I thought you just said—" Mia began.

"I like it," he said, padding it with cushions. "I'll make it fit into my house."

If only he could make Mia fit into his life as easily.

Chapter Thirteen

"I'LL HAVE THE chicken Caesar salad, please." Mia handed her menu to the young waiter and leaned back in her chair at the outdoor lakeside restaurant.

Blue water shimmered in a vast expanse, bounded by green hills dotted with tiny beaches and houses strung along the lakeshore. A flotilla of small sailing dinghies skimmed past, and closer to the rocky shore a pair of kayakers paddled leisurely.

She sighed quietly. How had a simple shopping trip turned into an emotional maelstrom? She loved spending time with Will, looked forward to every minute they were together and couldn't bear the thought of it ending. But while at times they managed the light and breezy affair she'd envisaged, at other times their emotional baggage dragged them under.

"I'll have the hot smoked beef sandwich with fries and coffee," Will said to the waiter.

Mia roused herself to dig in her tote for the cooler bag that held Billy's bottle. "Would you mind heating this up? A minute or two in the microwave."

"Yes, ma'am," the waiter said and left.

"This view is gorgeous," Mia said, determined not to let what happened at the antique store ruin the rest of the day. Because they surely had more to be glad than gloomy about. "You're lucky to have grown up around here."

Will noticed the sun was in Billy's eyes and adjusted the market umbrella. "I tend to take it for granted until I see it through a newcomer's eyes and realize how special it is."

"Have you always lived in Sweetheart?" she asked. "What kind of a name is that for a town, anyway?"

"Sweetheart is the name of the variety of cherries grown there," he said, resuming his seat. "And yep, born and bred locally."

"That must make you a Sweetheart," she teased, taking his hand beneath the table. His slow, sexy smile never failed to wake up the butterflies in her stomach.

He squeezed her hand then slid his fingers over her knee. "What do you say later we see if any of the cushions look good on your bed?" His voice was low and silky with sugges-tion, his eyes warm. "See how soft they are, and if they raise your hips nice and high."

A tingling started in her breasts. "Sounds good to me."

Will glanced at Billy, snoozing in his car seat. "Maybe we should wake him up or he won't sleep this afternoon."

"Good idea. Billy," she cooed softly as she gently picked him up. "Lunch time, sweetie." The waiter returned then with their drinks and Billy's warmed bottle. Mia shook it to mix the contents and tested it on her wrist. "Perfect. Thanks."

She tucked Billy into the crook of her arm and started to feed him. When her meal arrived she held the bottle with one hand and ate her salad with the other. Now and then she stole one of Will's fries with a cheeky smile.

"Hey!" he said, pretending to be outraged. "You're going to be in so much trouble when I get you home."

"Oh?" She eyed him sideways through lowered lashes. "What are you going to do to me?"

Before Will could reply, a woman called out, "Mia, is that you?" Shelley, her shiny blonde hair swinging from a high ponytail, crossed the deck toward them. Her low-cut sundress fit her slender figure like a glove and her heeled sandals made her legs look miles long.

Mia had only ever seen her in jeans or yoga pants and her glamorous transformation made her jaw drop. "Wow, you look great! Are you here for lunch?"

"That was my plan." Shelley leaned down to hug her and then brushed a hand over Billy's head. The baby smiled and kicked his feet. Then Shelley made a face. "My date called to cancel just as I got here."

"Join us," Mia said. "Will, this is Shelley, Laney's housemate and Billy's babysitter." To Shelley, she explained, "Will is Billy's godfather. We've just been up to the Flathead Shed to buy furniture for his new house and stuff for my apartment."

"Scoot over, Good-Lookin'." Shelley winked at Will then laughed at his surprised expression. "You don't recognize me, do you?"

"Um—" Will began.

"You sat behind me in Mr. Hooper's Grade Twelve English class." At Will's blank look, she added, "We did a project together on *Hamlet*."

"You're *that* Shelley?" Will said. "You've…changed."

Shelley turned to confide in Mia. "That's a polite way of saying I was a dog in high school. Acne, braces, frizzy hair—I had the works."

"It's hard to imagine you as anything but gorgeous," Mia said. "Especially now, seeing you all done up for a date."

The waiter came and Shelley ordered of a bowl of minestrone soup and a bread roll.

"I thought you moved away," Will said to her.

"I did," Shelley said. "I've been living in New York for most of the past ten years. Just got back a few months ago."

"What were you doing there?" he asked.

"I went hoping to become a stage actress and ended up a nanny." Shelley gave a self-deprecating smile. "But I was glad I failed at acting. I liked children so much I went on to study early childhood development at NYU."

"You didn't like the city enough to want to stay?" Mia asked. "I've only been once but I loved it."

"New York is great but, well, the old biological clock is

ticking." Shelley's soup arrived and she began to butter the roll. "I'm ready to settle down. I want to get married and raise my kids in Montana." She laughed. "All I need is to find a husband." Her gaze flicked to Will then away.

Mia blinked. Had Shelley just given Will the eye? She stabbed a piece of chicken and beat back a surge of jealousy. It was probably just a coincidence that Shelley happened to look Will's way right after she said that. Even if it wasn't, so what? Mia had been the one to say no strings. If he wanted to go out with other women he had every right to do so. She just hadn't thought the issue would come up this soon.

"Who was your date?" Mia put down her fork to wipe Billy's mouth with a napkin. "Anyone serious?"

"No, I met him online," Shelley said. "We haven't met in person yet and this is already the second time he's canceled on me at the last minute. I don't think I'll bother trying again." She turned to Will. "I heard about you and Katie breaking up and I'm so sorry. You two were, like, the perfect couple."

"Apparently not." Will spoke lightly but Mia could tell the question made him tense. His tapping fingers accidentally knocked her fork off the table.

Will looked around for the waiter but he wasn't in sight. Rising, he said, "I'll get you a new fork. And ask for more water while I'm at it."

Shelley watched him go inside the restaurant and then turned to Mia with a quizzical smile. "So…are you two together? Laney said not but she didn't sound too certain."

Mia hadn't said a word to Laney about her fling with Will because her sister couldn't keep a secret safe if she owned a bank vault. Now she stalled. "Why would you think that?"

"According to Laney you and Will are spending a lot of time together." Shelley shrugged. "He's single and hot. Why wouldn't you go for him?"

"I'm helping him decorate his house as a thank you for the help he's given me. Nothing more to it." Mia almost choked on the lie.

"Laney told me he delivered your baby," Shelley said. "How amazing is that?"

"Pretty amazing."

Shelley tore a piece off her roll and crumbled it. "So you wouldn't mind if I asked him out? I would never pursue a guy who was taken but if you two are just friends…"

Mia racked her brains but she couldn't think of one valid reason why she should prevent Shelley from asking Will out. Trying to be generous she told herself that Shelley might be just what Will was looking for. Kind and caring, she was ready to settle down in Sweetheart and start a family. And yet the thought of Will and Shelley together made Mia want to rip the other woman's heart out. Figuratively speaking.

"Just friends," Mia said, smiling brightly.

Will returned, bringing Mia a new fork and a bottle of water for the table.

"Say, Will," Shelley began, giving Mia a conspiratorial smile. "Some of our classmates from high school are organizing a mini reunion next Saturday at the tavern. Would you like to go together?"

"I heard about the reunion. Hadn't made up my mind to go or not." Will flicked Mia a glance, eyebrows raised.

"You should." Mia tried to infuse her voice with enthusiasm. "It sounds like fun."

"Doesn't that conflict with…that thing you wanted help with?" Will asked.

Jared's death anniversary. Hell. Will was determined to support her through it. Which was exactly what she didn't need, for him to see her at her most vulnerable, when she was most likely to let her guard down and cling to him for comfort, to accept whatever love he could give her. "I can handle it on my own."

"So you'll come to the reunion?" Shelley said to Will.

"Well…" he hedged.

"Please?" Shelley begged prettily, hands clasped. "I'd love to go with someone. It's been ages since I socialized with these people. I'm a little nervous."

Mia smiled at Will as hard as she could. She was not jealous. That would mean he mattered too much to her. "Go on. I mean it, honestly."

"I'll check my schedule and get back to you," he said to Shelley.

WILL DRUMMED HIS fingers on the open window frame of his truck as he drove back to Sweetheart. The breeze buffeting his face was scented with cherry blossoms from the orchards they were driving past and the lake sparkled under the spring sun. Mountains rose on his left, spectacular and wild, capped with snow. Normally he found this drive uplifting but today he was too jangled to notice the idyllic postcard scenery. Mia had practically thrown him at Shelley…

His gaze flicked to Mia with her exotic, silky dark hair, up-tilted amber eyes and rosy olive skin. She was still in love with her late husband, a man who had been larger than life. She'd said it herself, whenever Jared walked in the room, a party happened. They stayed in fancy hotels, lived the high life. By contrast did she think Will small-town and uninteresting? Right now she wanted a safe haven near her sister to raise her son. But how long would she be content in Sweetheart after being used to bigger things?

Will had been born and raised in Flathead Lake country and never had any desire to live anywhere else. He'd built his own home wanting to put down roots. The cherry trees he worked among literally anchored him to this land. Could Mia ever be happy long term with a guy from Sweetheart? Was that the real reason she didn't want to go public with their relationship? Was that why she was pushing him on to

Shelley?

"What's bugging you?" Mia said.

"Nothing."

"You're tapping incessantly. Something is wrong."

"I'm fine."

When Carmen had mistaken him for Billy's father there'd been a split second when he'd felt proud and happy. He'd wanted to *be* Billy's father, to ensure that the boy grew up feeling loved and accepted. So that Billy knew that even if his real father wasn't alive, he had a man who would raise him and never abandon him.

Wow. How much of that was his own inner abandoned child talking? No wonder Mia was wary of getting too close. He had issues he didn't even realize.

"Shelley's very pretty," Mia said. "And very nice."

"What was that about back there, anyway?" he said. "Are you trying to set me up?"

"I had nothing to do with Shelley's appearance at the restaurant." Mia's eyes flashed. "Why didn't you say yes to her? It's only a group of high school friends getting together."

"Is it?" He stretched his neck to get out the kinks brought on by tension. "Not that I think so highly of myself that I imagine every woman is after me now that I'm single but I can tell when a woman is interested."

Except when it came to Mia, who gave off so many mixed signals that she had him running around in circles.

Why would she sleep with him if she didn't feel something for him? She didn't strike him as the kind of woman who had sex with a lot of guys. On the other hand, why would she palm him off on Shelley if she wanted him? It didn't make sense.

Unless her motivation really was as simple as having a friend with benefits. His heart sank as he realized how much he'd hoped her feelings for him would eventually change to something more than friendship.

"Shelley's perfect for you," Mia argued. "She wants to settle down, she likes kids, all those things you said you wanted. She's even from Sweetheart so you have local history in common."

What if he wanted a dash of the outside world? He gripped the wheel to still his fingers. Keep it light; that's what Mia wanted. To hold on to her, he had to not let his true feelings show but store them under wraps.

And yet, he couldn't stop himself from saying, "Do you think you'll ever be able to love another man? I don't mean you should forget Jared. But will you ever let someone else into your heart?"

"You and I are not going to last, Will," she said sadly. "You'll work through your issues with me and then move on. That's what it means to be on the rebound."

Will saw a view point ahead and pulled into it. He cut the engine then twisted in his seat to face her. "Is that what you're doing? Working through your issues with me?"

She looked down at her hands, rubbing the bare spot on her ring finger where her wedding band had been. "I've struggled this past year, not just with debt but also mild anxiety and depression," she said finally. "I'm finally getting myself together again. I can't risk making another mistake. If I sink what would that mean for Billy? I don't want Nora and Jed to raise him."

"You've paid Jared's debts, you've got a job and an apartment, you're independent." Will ticked off her accomplishments on his fingers. "You've worked hard and you're a strong person. You're in a good place as far as I can see." He paused. "Sometimes you have to take a risk."

She played with the button on her jacket, twisting it back and forth. "I-I'm not ready."

She'd been through so much. What was he doing, browbeating her? "It's hard losing a partner the way you did," he said more gently. "But please, don't wrap yourself in widow's weeds forever. Keep your heart open."

Silently, she returned her gaze to the lake. Her sweet, heart-shaped face had that solemn expression he was getting to know all too well. The one that made him want to tickle her until she smiled again. The one he couldn't seem to break through no matter how hard he tried.

"Okay, maybe it's too soon for you to fall in love," Will went on. "But you're too full of life and joy to cut yourself off from it forever."

"You have no idea what I'm going through," she said

quietly.

"I haven't lost a loved one but I do know what it's like to have your world ripped out from under you," he said. "It's natural that you're afraid to give your heart again. You're a very special woman, Mia. I want you to be happy."

"I want you to be happy, too," Mia said, sounding on the verge of tears. "That's why I don't want to stop you from going out with Shelley. I've got too much baggage to contemplate anything other than a fling. And when the novelty of us wears off you'll realize you have years of dating to catch up on."

Here was his opportunity to tell her that he wasn't on the rebound, that he was fully over Katie. Then he remembered his reaction to being mistaken for Billy's father and doubt filled his mind. He wasn't even over his childhood trauma. How could he know for sure what feelings might still be lurking in his heart about Katie? Was anything ever simple?

He started the engine again and pulled back onto the road. Today had started out bright and full of fun—an adventure in his own backyard. He'd enjoyed watching Mia exclaim over an old figurine or an antiquated kitchen appliance, enjoyed her simple pleasure in the view from the restaurant. He'd thought a fling with her would be simple. Instead it was becoming more complicated daily. He could give her material assistance but he couldn't fix her broken heart. Not when she was so determined to be independent that she wouldn't trust him with her feelings.

And yet, along with the invisible barriers keeping them apart, invisible strings tied him to her, pulling them closer. Not the least of which was Billy.

In hindsight, he and Katie had had a kind of no-strings relationship. She'd been free to come and go; he to see other women while she was away. It hadn't worked. She'd finally figured that out and ended it whereas he might have gone on indefinitely the way they were. What did that say about him? Had he been so determined not to be his father, and not to abandon a woman he'd once loved, that he'd clung to an outdated relationship?

When he came to the crossroads he slowed. "Do you want to go home or come to my place?"

Mia glanced in the back at Billy. He was awake but restless from a long day, batting fretfully at the toys dangling from his car seat. "I'll have a quiet night if you don't mind."

"If you feel like a movie on Netflix later, give me a buzz."

She nodded noncommittally. Something was wrong between them and he had no idea what it was, much less how to fix it. Helplessness made him frustrated. After only a few months of knowing her, he was falling for her, hard. He wanted strings, damn it.

A few minutes later he pulled up in front of her apartment. He got out and unhooked Billy's car seat for her. "So do you want me to go out with Shelley?"

"It's not about what *I* want," she said. "If you want to, go ahead."

He was about to kiss her goodbye when a car pulled into the parking lot. He touched her arm instead, furious at the situation they'd created where he couldn't show her how much he cared. "See you later."

"Say bye-bye, Billy." She waved Billy's hand for him.

Will climbed back in his truck and continued home. Mia cared about him as a friend. She made love with him but he had to accept the possibility that she might never *love* him heart and soul.

The way he was starting to love her.

Chapter Fourteen

"LANEY, THERE'S SOMETHING wrong with Billy." Mia tucked the phone into her ear and tried to settle the red-faced, squalling baby against her shoulder but he wouldn't relax. "Every night this week, he has his evening bottle and seems perfectly fine. Then just as I'm about to put him to bed for the night, he starts howling and won't stop for hours."

"No diaper pin sticking into him?" Laney said.

"He's wearing a disposable. I checked all his clothing. Nothing's twisted or too tight. He's fed, he's changed. There's no reason on earth I can see why he should be crying."

"I'll ask Shelley," Laney said. "Maybe she knows."

Through her worry over Billy, Mia registered that Shelley was home, and not out with Will. No, dammit, she didn't want him to go out with Shelley but she'd painted herself into a corner with her no-strings stipulation. She hadn't foreseen how much it would matter to her if he did date other women, how hard she would fall for him. She sighed.

Which meant it was time to let him go.

Shelley came on the line. "Does Billy have a fever, vomiting or diarrhea?"

Mia felt his forehead. It was warm because he'd worked himself into a sweat but he didn't feel feverish. "None of those."

"Do all his body parts look normal? Was he behaving normally earlier?"

"Yes and yes." Mia paced, jiggling the baby in her arms.

"It sounds as if he has colic," Shelley said. "Usually that happens with younger babies but it's not unheard of at Billy's age. It's perfectly normal."

"Should I take him to Emergency?"

"No, just walk him around or put him in a buggy and push him," Shelley suggested. "Sometimes driving in the car helps."

"You're sure there's nothing seriously wrong?" Mia asked.

"Positive. He should calm down in an hour or two."

An hour or two? Mia didn't know how much more of this she, or Billy, could take. "Thanks."

She bundled Billy up warmly and loaded him into the car then drove aimlessly around the darkened streets of the town, out to Route 35 and back again. While the car was moving he stopped crying but every time she slowed at an intersection he started up again. She headed back down Finley Road. The Starr Orchards were lovely in the moonlight, the white blossoms glowing against the black sky. Between the branches, stars glittered. Mia sang along to country and western songs on the radio, hoping her voice would lull Billy to sleep.

Somehow she ended up on the gravel road that led to Will's house. His lights were on and his truck was in the car port. She slowed, then stopped at the end of the driveway, wondering whether she should go in. Instinctively she'd headed for the person who always made her feel safe and loved. Who even when they were at odds, she could count on to be there for her.

Billy, quiet a moment ago, started crying again, tossing his blankets and kicking. Will had said she could come to him if she ever needed anything. Even so, she didn't feel right about bringing him a crying baby, especially since they hadn't parted on particularly good terms the other day.

"Please, stop, Billy." Mia felt wetness on her cheeks and realized she was crying, too. She was about to drive away when the front door opened.

"Mia?" Will crossed the yard in long strides. "What's wrong? Is Billy okay?"

"He's got colic," she said. "Sorry to disturb you. I'm just driving around, hoping he'll settle."

"Come inside," Will said.

"I'll tough it out." As supportive as Will was she couldn't expect him to take this on.

Ignoring her, Will opened the rear door and picked up

the screaming baby, trailing blankets. "Come here, you little rascal. You shouldn't upset your mom. She's the one who feeds you." He turned to Mia. "I'll make hot chocolate."

Mia gave up protesting and grabbed her purse gratefully. "You do know the way to a girl's heart."

Billy quieted to a low-level fussing as Will led the way into the living room. "The couch came today," he said. "What do you think of the new upholstery? I took your suggestion on the fabric."

She sank onto the couch which he'd had recovered in dark brown raw silk, and ran her hand over the textured fabric. The vintage curves of the scalloped back went beautifully with the smooth river stones of the fireplace and he'd used the orange silk cushions as bright accents. "I love it." She noticed a teak mantelpiece had appeared over the fireplace. "Where did you get that? It's beautiful."

"I made it." Will laid Billy tummy down over his splayed hand and forearm. Billy took a deep shuddering breath, hiccupped and fell silent, his arms and legs dangling limply.

"*What the?* You are a baby whisperer," Mia said. "How did you do that?"

Will swung Billy in a gentle arc and his eyelids drooped. "One of my friends does this with his baby when she cries. How long since you've had a decent night's sleep?"

"What day is it?" she retorted wearily.

Will started to lay Billy on the couch next to her but he startled awake and started crying again. "That settles it. You go lie down on my bed. I'll bring your hot drink and then you can rest while I walk Mr. Vocal Cords here."

Mia was too tired to protest. She let Will take her arm and guide her down the hall to the bedroom. She would just close her eyes for a few minutes…

WILL SET MIA'S drink on the nightstand. He pulled up the quilt and then brushed back a strand of hair from her face. Sleeping Beauty. Was this the last time she would ever lie in his bed? Billy began to fuss again so Will carried him back to the living room. The baby was exhausted, too, but stubbornly refusing to nod off.

Finally, after an hour of pacing between the kitchen and the living room, up and down the hall, Billy closed his eyes. His Cupid's bow mouth worked, a tiny frown puckering his forehead, and then gradually his face relaxed into the smoothness of sleep. Carefully, Will sat on the couch. Peace at last.

Will gazed fondly at the baby. Little stinker. Out of nowhere, an ache rose in his chest. This poor fatherless child. He wanted to make a difference in Billy's life, to be a loving, reliable male figure. He and Mia could be so good together. But he had to face facts, they weren't on the same page. She was still grieving for Jared and while she might enjoy Will's company she wasn't ready to move on emotionally.

So much for his New Year's resolution not to fall in love again. That seemed like a million years ago now. Keeping the resolution should have been easy. It wasn't like he fell in love at the drop of a hat. In the past ten years there'd only been Katie whom he considered he really loved. During Katie's years away there'd been other women, but no one serious.

Until Mia. From the get go he'd felt so sure they had a special bond. She'd warned him a relationship was a mistake and he hadn't listened. Oh, no. He'd thought he would be the guy to bring her back to life after her husband died. To make her feel loved again. What he hadn't counted on was finding out that he was vulnerable.

There was no point in pretending that she would fall in love with him. He needed to protect himself. If they kept seeing each other, he would end up hurt. Well, so he would hurt. He didn't care. Even knowing what he knew now, he would do it all again. But they couldn't go on as they were—that much was clear.

He rose and carried Billy into the bedroom. The cherry box was propped against the wall where Mia had left it the last time she'd come over. Will made a nest in it with a throw and laid Billy down. The baby had grown so much he was almost too big. Will undressed except for his boxers and got into bed next to Mia. He kissed her temple lightly and rolled away. With her lying next to him it took a long time for him to fall asleep.

When he woke, just after dawn, Mia's arm was around

his waist and she was snugged up against his back. Will listened for Billy and heard him breathing, a little congested from all his crying, but still asleep. Gently, he laid his hand over Mia's. If only he could slow down time and they could stay like this indefinitely…

Mia stirred to life and smoothed her hand over his chest. "Make love to me," she whispered.

His groin tightened. "I'm not sure that's a good idea."

"Please."

One last time. The unspoken words hung between them.

"Never could refuse a request from you," he said, and turning, took her in his arms. Her kiss was all the sweeter because their days were suddenly numbered. She moved against him, her body soft and languid with sleep. He lowered a hand to her breast and felt the warmth and softness. "Mia…"

"Mmm, don't talk." Her eyes were closed and her hands were moving down his back, lower and lower to knead the muscles of his butt. "You feel so good."

"I need to say something."

Mia opened her eyes. "What is it?"

It was so quiet he could hear the clock ticking away the seconds. "If I go out with Shelley, us sleeping together wouldn't be right. I'm done with that kind of relationship."

A long beat went by. "I understand. And I agree." She pulled her top over her head.

Will undid the snap on her jeans and she slid them

down. Bra and panties fell off the side of the bed. He removed his boxers and tossed them, too. In the faint light of early morning they lay on their sides and gazed at each other. Delicately, he traced the contours of her breasts with a fingertip. No strings. What a load of shit that term was. Invisible ropes of affection and respect and longing bound them together. Billy was caught in the web, too, meshing the three of them tighter than he could ever have expected.

Mia kissed the hard muscle of his pecs, inhaling the warmth and musk of his skin. "I'm going to miss how you smell."

"Don't talk about missing me, or last times," he said gruffly.

"You're right. This is supposed to be fun. Let's get sexy." She reached down and took him in her hand. His cock sprang to life. "So hard, so quickly," she marveled.

"I do like your breasts." He took them in both his hands and pushed them up so he could take her nipples into his mouth, one at a time, bringing them to glistening peaks. Then he worked his way down to her belly and her hips, not missing an inch of her delicious curves. He concentrated fiercely on loving her to stop himself from thinking about losing her.

She stifled a moan when he nudged her knees apart and licked between her legs. They were trying to be quiet so as not to wake Billy and the enforced silence seemed to increase the intensity. Hushed whispers and muffled moans when he wanted her screaming with lust. He wanted to drive himself into her, stake her to his bed and never let her go. This could be their last time together. That, combined with the tension of not knowing if they'd be interrupted, gave an extra urgency, almost a desperation to their lovemaking. And an added piquancy to every kiss, every touch.

When he had her on the brink of coming, she dragged him up and captured his mouth. "I'm ready. I want you inside me."

He was ready, too, but he wished he wasn't. He wanted to make this moment last forever. Outside, the birds started trilling and cooing. A rooster crowed in the distance. Morning was coming. Soon they would have to get up and go their separate ways.

He reached into a drawer for a condom and put it on. Her eyes fluttered closed; her lips parted as he pushed into her. "Look at me."

She opened her amazing eyes and speared his soul. Mia. He couldn't pinpoint the exact moment when he'd fallen in love with her but that love was a bottomless pit and there was no way out. Too soon, he felt the pleasure spiraling out of control. Their bodies strained together as if they would meld. At the peak, there was no Will, no Mia. Only the two of them together as one, riding a blazing star that soared through the heavens.

Inevitably, the comet burned out. Gently, slowly, Will fell back to earth, broken and alone.

WILL THREW A match on the cherry tree prunings piled high in the bare dirt behind the packing shed and soaked in fire starter. Flames burst into life, licking the sky. The spring ritual that he normally regarded as just another chore now seemed cathartic.

"Hey." Garret crossed the yard from the packing shed. "You started without me."

"I'm done with wasting time." Will snapped a branch over his knee with a sharp crack and chucked both pieces into the inferno. Looking back over the past few months was like watching a train wreck in slow motion. All the way he'd been too eager, too ready to go along with whatever scraps Mia had thrown him.

Garret pushed up the sleeves of his russet-colored sweater and picked up unlit branches to slot into glowing holes in the burning pile. "Not like you to be impatient. Something wrong?"

"Mia." Using a long stick, Will poked a branch, sending showers of sparks flying.

"Ah," Garret said with a wealth of understanding.

Will glanced over his shoulder at the empty orchard and the deserted lane. "Don't tell anyone what I'm about to say. It's a secret."

"You and Mia are having an affair?" Garret surmised.

Will's head came around sharply. "How did you know?"

"I saw her leaving your place the other morning, early. She didn't see me but I saw her."

"Have you told anyone?"

"No." Garret's dark eyes were sympathetic. "I figured if you wanted people to know you'd be open about it."

"The secrecy was her idea," Will said. "She didn't think we would last so she got me to agree to a no-strings affair."

"She used you, bro. No wonder you're angry."

"She didn't use me. I went in with my eyes open. If I'm pissed at anyone, it's myself."

Garret picked up more branches and threw them on. The flames spit and crackled. "She was crying that morning I saw her if it makes you feel any better."

"It doesn't. I don't want her to be sad." Even if their relationship wouldn't last the distance, their time together had been special. He wanted them both to remember it with pleasure and affection. "But it's over. I'm going to support her through the anniversary of her late husband's death. Then that's it. She says we have no future and I'm not going to beat my head against a brick wall."

"What about Billy?" Garret dragged the root ball of an old tree over and heaved it on. Flames shot skyward.

Will stepped back from the heat of the eight-foot blaze. "I'll always be Billy's godfather. I just won't see him as often. Which is probably a good thing right now."

They watched the blaze for a while in silence.

"I saw posters up around town about your high school

reunion at the tavern," Garret asked. "Are you going?"

"Shelley Powers asked me to go with her," Will said. "She doesn't know about me and Mia."

Garret twisted his even features into a pained expression. "Dude, what is it about you that all these hot women are after you? I had a such a crush on Shelley in high school." He sighed. "The 'older' woman."

"Funny, I barely remembered her," Will said. "She said she had braces and acne."

"Well, yeah, but also a cute smile and a great body," Garret said. "Are you going with her?"

"I don't know." Will shook his head. "I'm happy to take her so she'll have someone to walk in with but I don't want to mislead her." He looked at Garret. "Why don't you come with us?"

Garret brightened then shook his head. "Nah, but maybe I'll drop in for a drink." He warmed his hands at the fire. "So are you still bummed out about Katie?"

"I've made peace with that," Will said. "I was hanging on to her for the wrong reasons."

No, he was bummed about losing Mia. He still thought she must love him just a little. If she gave him a chance, it might grow into something big. But as long as she kept pushing him away, that would never happen.

Chapter Fifteen

THE MORNING OF the first anniversary of Jared's death, Mia awoke at dawn filled with a vague sadness. Lying in bed thinking made it worse so she got up and put coffee on and moved about the apartment, getting herself organized. Thank goodness Will had insisted on spending the day with her. She hadn't thought she would need him to hold her hand but it turned out she did.

She got Billy up and took him out to the living room to feed him his bottle. The sky over the tops of the town's buildings was clear, heralding the beginning of a fine day. In contrast, on this day a year ago, it had rained in Billings. The soldiers who came to her door wore rain ponchos that had dripped on her foyer. There'd been two: a woman with short dark hair in sergeant's stripes and a younger man of some junior rank. Mia remembered his eyes, the way he watched her, grave and pitying, while his senior officer gave her the terrible news.

Her legs had given way, she recalled, and she'd uttered a single despairing 'no.' The woman had steered her to the couch and the young man brought a glass of water. She'd sat there in a numb haze, clutching the glass. Fragments of sentences had penetrated the fog. Killed in action…died saving others…hero.

Now, Mia wiped her wet eyes with the heel of her hand. The grand gesture was so like Jared. Getting killed was not. He must have been royally peeved when he realized—if he'd had time to be aware—that he wasn't going to get bailed out of this scrape. Mia gave a ragged laugh. Damn him, anyway.

Billy gurgled around the teat of the bottle, laughing because she had. Oh, baby. Tears fell then of regret, pain and loss. The life and death of Jared Richards had been one enormous, continuous churn of emotion. She was so tired, so very, very tired of feeling.

Until Will had come along. He'd brought light and laughter back into her life. And she'd pushed him away. Was she making an enormous mistake? What if he was the real thing? But no, no one left a ten-year relationship without significant baggage. No one built a house for a woman and then was okay with her not moving in. Will was stoical, good at covering pain or discomfort with a smile. Sometimes what looked and felt like moving on was just the heart tricking you into not feeling the pain of your breakup.

Last night he'd sent a text telling her he would pick her up early in the morning. They'd messaged back and forth, making arrangements. Other than that, she hadn't seen or spoken to him since the night Billy had colic and she'd stayed over. She'd deliberately kept away and she knew he was busy in the orchard. Billy still cried every night for hours but some over the counter drops helped and thanks to Will she'd learned tricks to calm her baby.

But at night, when she was alone, all she could think of was Will. Somehow, in spite of her best intentions, she'd ended up being his rebound fling. If he and Shelley hit it off, and if Mia kept Billy in Shelley's childcare, which she wanted to do, she would be bound to see Will on a regular basis. She couldn't have devised a more excruciating scenario for herself if she'd tried.

That last morning together had been hard. Both of them had lavished attention on Billy so they didn't have to see the anguish in each other's eyes.

"All done, sweetie?" Mia wiped Billy's mouth and raised him to her shoulder, patting his back. She finished eating a cold piece of toast and drinking her coffee and then changed Billy. After packing a lunch she dressed in hiking gear and boots as instructed by Will. Somehow she would get through this day. It wasn't remembering Jared that would be so hard. It was knowing this would be the last day she'd spend alone with Will. She planned to savor every minute.

She'd dropped Billy off at Laney's house and was waiting outside with her daypack when Will's truck rumbled to a stop. Between Shelley and Laney, Billy would be well looked after until Mia got home.

"Where are we going?" she asked as they drove off. He'd

been mysterious about the day's activity, only saying they were going hiking.

At the end of Sweet Street Will turned down 1st Street, then made a right on Mission Range Road, heading east toward the mountains. "Have you ever seen an alpine meadow in spring?"

"Can't say as I have." She looked toward the soaring white-tipped peaks of the Mission Range not fifty miles away. She'd started doing yoga and jogging again but was she fit enough for a prolonged hike? Only half-joking, she said, "Please tell me we're taking a helicopter."

It was bittersweet that in spite of the tension between them, she easily slipped into their casual, intimate way of talking. Almost as if nothing was wrong.

"How are you holding up?" He started to reach out to touch her knee, then rested his hand on the gear stick instead.

She saw the movement and her heart felt sore. Could she really do this? "I'm okay. Honestly. If you had other things you needed to do today, that would be all right. I'm not going to fall apart."

"Don't speak too soon," he said. "Death anniversaries can sneak up on you."

Curious, she glanced at him. "That sounds like the voice of experience."

"My grandmother died when I was ten years old," Will told her. "I didn't think it affected me much until that summer when we made our annual trip to my grandparents' farm. When I walked into their kitchen and there was no scent of pies baking or the sound of her welcoming voice that's when it hit me she was gone for good." His jaw worked. "I felt so lost that summer and to this day August holds sad memories."

"I'm sorry." Mia touched his arm. Just because they weren't going to be together didn't mean she'd stopped caring. Will was right, though. The death of a loved one didn't hit all at once. Memories snuck up when least expected and sorrow could last for years. Or so the army psychologist had counseled her. However, discovering Jared's infidelity had killed the last vestige of her love for him. She was sorry he'd died and if she could bring him back to life, she would. But she was tired of feeling sad, and tired of feeling guilty because she didn't feel sadder.

She put on her sunglasses and watched the mountains coming closer. She needed to not think about what she'd lost, either Jared—her baby's father—or with Will. Look forward, not back. Outward, not in. Today she would feel the sun on her face, hear the wind, smell the damn wild flowers. Winter was over. It was about time spring began.

They crossed Route 35 and continued on Mission Range Road into the mountains. The air flowing in the open window was cool and scented with pine.

She was dying to ask him the questions that so far she'd restrained herself from asking Shelley. Had he called the other woman? What had she said? Were they going to dinner before the reunion? She wanted to know even though hearing the details would be like probing a sore tooth.

"Will there be bears?" she asked instead.

"I've hiked in these mountains all my life and only encountered grizzlies a handful of times."

"O-kay. That's…reassuring." Not. She waited for him to say he'd packed a bear stun gun or that it was too early in the season but got nothing. Knowing Will, though, he would be prepared.

They turned off Mission Range Road onto a gravel road of sharp switchbacks that climbed steadily, back and forth, up and up. Mia held on to the strap and braced herself for the corners. The road became narrower until it petered out in a small parking area where the trail began. They donned daypacks loaded with water and food, hats and light jackets.

Mia followed Will into the forest. Shards of light broke through the branches overhead making a dappled pattern on the carpet of pine needles. The trail climbed around massive boulders, over swiftly flowing creeks and through dark stands of tall trees. Before long Mia had forgotten about bears and Shelley and Jared and concentrated simply on putting one foot in front of the other. Her breath came in huffs as she taxed her legs and lungs with the steep climb.

Ahead of her on the path, Will hiked in silence. His blue chambray shirt became stained with sweat down the back. They paused a couple of times for a drink of water but conversation was limited to strictly utilitarian exchanges. An hour passed, then two, then three. Gradually, the trees thinned out. They emerged onto a sunny, sloping meadow that stretched around the curving side of the mountain and up toward the peak for a few hundred yards.

Mia stopped in her tracks, blown away. The mountainside was ablaze with wild flowers. Lupins and snowdrops, Indian paintbrush and daisies and flowers she couldn't identify. Pinks and yellows and delicate blues, white and purple and gently waving green grass.

"This is breathtaking." She turned to Will to share her delight. "I've never seen anything so beautiful. Thank you for bringing me here."

"I thought you'd like it." His eyes had never looked so blue as they did next to the big Montana sky. His hair shone like gold in the spring sunshine and his smile magnified her buoyant mood.

Was it wrong to feel happy on the anniversary of Jared's death? If so, she couldn't help it and she wasn't going to waste time fighting it. Life was complicated like that, never just one emotion at a time.

"Let's eat," she said, to steer her mind away from guilty thoughts. "I'm starving."

They walked higher to sit on flat rocks where they could gaze out over the meadow down to the valley below. The town of Sweetheart, farm fields, orchards, houses along the lakeshore. And the whole of Flathead Lake, shining and blue.

Mia pulled sandwiches from her backpack. Will poured them both coffee from a thermos. She ate a turkey and cheese roll in silence, enjoying the breeze on her damp neck. Tall white clouds floated majestically across the blue sky like ships in full sail. When the world was this beautiful surely things couldn't be all bad.

Lying on his side, Will looked up at her. "What are you thinking?"

"Just counting my blessings. I survived this past year. I have a beautiful baby, a job, a home, family and friends." She looked down at the sandwich in her hands. "You came into my life."

"We had fun." His smile flashed and then was gone. Sitting up, he crumpled his sandwich wrapping and tucked it in the backpack. "More coffee?"

"Will…" Mia began. If they were breaking up she didn't want them to part on a lie. Will was the best thing that had ever happened to her and he deserved the truth. "Jared wasn't the wonderful guy I thought I married." Will went very still which somehow made it harder for her to go on. But go on, she must. "That good guy image was a sham. For the whole of this last year I've pretended that I still thought he was amazing, and that I loved him. I did it for Billy's sake so he wouldn't grow up knowing what a jerk his father was."

"A jerk?" The word seemed to galvanize Will. Frowning, he said, "But I thought…"

"I stopped loving Jared long before he died," she continued, determined to tell everything before getting sidetracked with details. "At one time I'd hoped we could salvage our marriage but when he left for Iraq it was pretty much over; I just didn't want to admit it. Then he was killed and a hero, and I thought why bring up all the bad stuff?"

"What bad stuff?" Will said. "I can't believe you've never said anything like this before."

"A few months ago…" Her voice cracked, remembering the damning text messages. "I found out he'd been cheating on me."

Will's mouth flattened. "Go on." There was a hard edge to his voice.

It should have occurred to her that maybe not all Will's anger was directed at Jared but all she could think of was how much time she'd wasted protecting Jared's image. How thoroughly she'd suppressed her finer emotions for the sake of a man who'd wronged her in just about every way possible.

Mia scrambled to her feet, unable to sit still. The outrage and resentment she'd kept locked up inside for so long poured out. "I hate him for what he did to me," she said loudly, fists clenched. "Jared Richards was a selfish, entitled, lying, thieving, cheating son of a bitch!" The last few words reverberated off the rocky mountain side.

She sat back down, stunned at her own outburst. She'd never even acknowledged half those things to herself, let alone anyone else. She'd always tried to see the best in the man, to preserve some good feelings for him for the sake of her son. Tried to make herself believe that she hadn't been criminally stupid in her choice of husband. Speaking the truth felt good. Letting all her anger out at last was cathartic.

She turned to Will, elated and grinning. But if she thought he would be glad she wasn't grieving she'd been mistaken. Instead his face wore a thunderous scowl. Her smile faded. "What's the matter?"

"You *hated* him?" Now Will got to his feet and loomed over her. "He was a son of a bitch? You've been lying to me all these months? What about the hero part? Did he really save those soldiers?"

"Yes, that part's true." She flinched at the force of Will's anger, so unlike his usual easygoing, good humor. "I-I could show you his medal."

"I don't want to see his goddamn medal." Will's nostrils flared as if he was fighting to contain his emotions. "When you lost your house, was it because he screwed up somehow?" Biting her lip, she nodded. "And he did other seriously bad things, maybe dishonest things?" She nodded again, the sick feeling in her stomach growing. "And he cheated on you, too?"

"Yes." She realized too late that she should have eased into the truth instead of getting carried away and blurting it out. It was too much to share all at once. She got to her feet again and faced him. "I'm sorry, Will. You have a right to be angry. I did lie to you but I-I didn't mean anything bad by it."

Will wasn't at all pacified by her apology. "If you didn't love him, why did you keep pushing me away?" he demanded. "No matter how much fun we had together, or how much pleasure we gave each other, or how profoundly meaningful our encounters, you never believed it would work. Do you feel *anything* for me?"

Mia winced. He wasn't just angry, he was also hurt. Again, as he had every right to be. "Of course I feel something for you. You've been a wonderful friend and so good to Billy. I love you like a—"

"Do not say like a brother." He stabbed a finger at her. "You were in my bed the other night. We made love."

"Not like a brother, no, of course not." Hell. She felt awful. She would rather confront a grizzly than acknowledge how badly she'd treated this wonderful man. In fact, she wouldn't blame Will if he fed her to the bears. She turned away, unable to face his accusing glare. "I was protecting myself," she said in a small voice. "You're on the rebound. Rebound affairs never last. I told you we shouldn't get involved. I warned you we wouldn't last. And we haven't."

"You made that happen!" he roared. "If I'd had my way we would have been living together by now."

The hairs stood up on the back of her neck. There it was. Proof, if she'd needed it. Diving into a new relationship too fast was among the top three rebound symptoms. She turned around slowly. "Don't you think that's a little soon?"

He blinked, his shocked silence acknowledging she was right.

Angry, remorseful, not knowing what to think or feel, Mia strode up the mountain, wading through meadow grass, crushing wild flowers. Up and up, to the line of boulders that marked the beginning of the glacial moraine. She could barely catch her breath in the thin air.

Will came after her and stopped a few feet away. "I'm sorry I yelled," he said stiffly. "I don't normally do that."

She pressed her hands against the rough granite at her back for strength and reached deep, searching for the truth of her own feelings and motivation. "You were with Katie for a decade and couldn't commit to her. Why would I believe you would commit to me?"

Will went pale beneath his tan. "You and Katie are very different people."

"So, what, you like me because I'm different to Katie? In what way? I'm brunette while she's a blonde? She's tall and I'm short? Don't you see what happened?" Mia cried. "You were devastated at losing your fiancée and your dream of having children. Along I come, with a baby whom you deliver." She waved a hand. "It's Fate. The Universe is speaking to you. We have a bond. You have a ready-made family."

"The Universe didn't speak to me," Will said. "Your smile did. Your eyes. You."

"If you're trying to make up to Billy for what you suffered as a child, maybe what you feel for me isn't love," Mia went on, hurt now herself. "I'm your rebound fling, the one you forget after you've healed and moved on." She dragged in a shuddering breath. "I can't do this anymore. It's too hard on Billy. He's already in love with you."

And by Billy, she meant herself, too.

Will dragged both hands roughly through his hair. "Even if I am on the rebound, it doesn't mean my feelings for you aren't real."

"I can't take that chance," she whispered, tears welling.

"And I can't get through to you." He gave her a long look of anger and regret, sorrow and frustration. "Maybe Shelley would be better suited to me, after all."

Mia leaned against the boulder and closed her eyes. Just as she'd feared, the worst had happened. She'd lost him. She'd kept pushing him away and finally he'd given up. She'd just ruined the best thing that had ever happened to her. Why had she done that? Didn't she think she deserved to be happy? What was wrong with her? Why was she so afraid?

"WHAT WOULD YOU like to drink?" Will spoke into Shelley's ear to be heard over the loud music.

Their reunion party was taking place in the bar at the heritage-listed Montreau Hotel. Considering that their original graduation party had been around a fire pit in the Starr Orchards, the hotel's polished wood, gleaming brass fittings and crystal chandelier were a tad more upmarket. About thirty people had shown up out of their graduating class of fifty-odd, some coming from as far away as Bozeman and Marietta. One of their class members had designated himself DJ and put together a playlist of popular songs from their day.

"White wine, please." Shelley regarded him with a faint smile, her expression both quizzical and wistful. "I get the feeling you're not really into this party. Or maybe it's me you're not into?"

The toe of Will's polished leather shoe beat a tattoo on the hardwood floor. Shelley was pretty, smart and interested in him. She wasn't pushing him away, that's for sure. If Mia was right, he'd done his rebound phase with her and he was ready to move on. But he didn't think his path had followed the conventional theory. In hindsight he'd been over Katie long before their actual relationship had ended.

"I've been seeing someone but it's not working out," he admitted. "I should be upfront, though. I'm not ready for anything new. I shouldn't have asked you out tonight."

"It's okay," Shelley said. "I sensed your hesitation even when I invited you. I'm glad you came with me, though." She held out a hand. "Friends?"

"Friends," Will said gratefully, clasping her hand.

"Is it Mia?" she asked, releasing his hand.

"Did Laney say something?" So much for secrecy.

Shelley shook her head. "It's obvious by the way you two look at each other when you think no one is noticing."

"Well, whatever we had, it's over." He still couldn't believe their liaison had ended so abruptly and with such finality. "I'll get your wine."

Will made his way to the bar. A few years ago he would have considered a no-strings affair to be fine. But it wasn't what he wanted anymore. As for his attachment to Billy, in the beginning there might have been some truth in what Mia said about him mourning his lost opportunity to have a family with Katie. But now that he knew Billy, he loved the kid for his own sake. And the Universe *had* spoken to him. He couldn't explain it, but he believed it. He and Mia were meant to be together.

All the old gang was here tonight. He nodded to his cousins—Jess, Carrie, Jacie—and their partners. Out on the dance floor Alex and Emma were swinging to a golden oldie. Emma had grown up across the street from Will and had been like part of the family since they were kids. Until a year ago Alex had been a high-flying advertising and marketing guru in Seattle. Now he fit right into life in Sweetheart. Mia could fit in here, too. If she wanted to.

"Two Rivers ale," he said to the bartender, naming a local craft beer. "And a Chardonnay."

"Hey." Garret slapped him on the back. "Where's your date?"

"Shelley's over there." Will nodded to the far side of the room where she was chatting to girlfriends. "Although we just established that this isn't actually a date."

"You don't say." Garret dragged his gaze from Shelley and ordered a beer, then said to Will, "How did things go with Mia up on the mountain?"

"Not great," Will said tersely. He understood Mia's fear of getting hurt again but he couldn't condone the lies. He'd been lied to too many times in his life about critical things. First his father keeping his secret family hidden, then Katie not telling him about Marcus...

The surge of anger over Katie's treatment of him brought him up short. When he'd told Mia about Katie sleeping with Marcus while they were together he'd brushed it off as not that important. He'd never drilled down past the humiliation and hurt to the anger he felt. It wasn't simply that Katie had fallen in love with Marcus. *She hadn't told Will about the other man.* She'd lied by omission. She'd let him go on believing they still had a long-distance thing going on months after she'd known it was over.

"What happened up there?" Garret asked, pulling him back to their conversation about Mia.

Will opened his mouth to tell him about Jared, then stopped. Mia had a point about not spreading rumors about Billy's father. The man was dead. What good would it do to blacken his name, especially if it might harm Billy?

"We broke it off. According to Mia we have too much

baggage." The bartender handed across the drinks and Will gave him his credit card. "Do you think I have baggage?"

"Everyone over the age of twenty-five has baggage of some sort." Garret nodded to the entrance. "Speaking of which."

Will looked over and saw Katie enter, cool and lovely, her blonde hair gathered in an elegant knot at her nape. Seeing her now confirmed that he didn't love her the way he used to, long ago. And he was over his hurt and humiliation. But he hadn't forgiven her.

"I'll take Shelley her wine," Garret said. "If you want a word with Katie."

"Yeah, thanks, that would be good," Will said.

Katie came up to him and put her evening bag on the bar. "Good turnout. How are you?"

"Fine," he said, coolly. "Where's Marcus?"

"In Marietta on business." She glanced around. "Where's Mia?"

Will rubbed at a peeling corner on the beer label. "Why does everyone think she and I are a couple?"

"Come on, Will. It's obvious." Her smile faded as she took in his grim expression. "What is it?"

"Why didn't you tell me about Marcus?" he demanded. "We regularly sent each other texts and emails. We saw each other a couple of times last year. I'm not angry that you fell in love with him. I'm angry that you never told me. I thought we were friends." Just as he'd thought he and Mia were friends.

"I know, I should have been more considerate of your feelings." Katie shrugged unhappily, one arm wrapped protectively around her waist. "I was scared of stepping off the ledge, I guess. I knew I loved Marcus but I'd known you nearly all my life. I was hedging my bets, wanting to be absolutely certain before I let you go. It wasn't until you were proposing that I realized that was wrong." She swallowed and looked away. "I hated to hurt you."

"Lies hurt more than any truth," he said.

Her mouth twisted. "Haven't you ever been less than honest?"

"I—" he began, ready to defend his integrity, then stopped. What right had he to be self-righteous when he'd let Mia think he was on the rebound and pining over Katie? Hell, Mia still thought that. He'd castigated her for lying but he hadn't been totally honest, either. They'd both been so busy protecting their bruised hearts that they hadn't trusted each other.

"What were you going to say?" Katie asked.

"Never mind. People in glass houses... I'm working through some things." He met her gaze with a rueful smile and realized that he didn't need to have it out with her. Just recognizing his feelings had closed that chapter in his life. "I wish you and Marcus the best, I really do."

"You're a good guy, Will." She hesitated. "Are you still going to come to my wedding?"

"Wouldn't miss it," he said. "Listen, I've got to go. Enjoy the party."

He wove through the people ringing the dance floor to say goodbye to Shelley and to make sure she had a ride home. Garret offered instantly and Will didn't think she minded too much.

Now, he had to find Mia and convince her that their love was real.

Chapter Sixteen

M IA HELD BILLY long after he'd fallen asleep purely for the comfort of his solid warm little body next to hers. Then she laid him next to her on the couch and reached for a square of green origami paper and began folding it into a boat shape with a flat bottom.

Try as she might, she couldn't stop going over the day on the mountain. The descent had been swift, tense and silent. Mia had brushed off Will's stilted suggestion that he stay with her for the rest of the evening and insisted he go to the party with Shelley. It was over. No more conflicting emotions, no more fighting her desires and impulses. Now she could concentrate on work and Billy and saving for a house of her own without the distraction of a love affair that would only leave her heartbroken in the end.

She should have been happy. Instead she was miserable.

But she'd done the right thing. Hadn't she?

Laney hadn't thought so. After Will had dropped Mia off at her sister's, Laney had taken one look at Mia's strained, tear-stained face and pulled her into a long hug. Even then

Mia had kept up a facade until she'd learned that Shelley was at the Beauty Spot getting her hair done for the party. Then she'd spilled out the whole saga of first her and Jared, and then her and Will.

Laney had been sympathetic rather than judgmental but she hadn't bought Mia's insistence that Will deserved more than Mia could offer. Instead she'd asked tough questions. "Do you distrust Will? Do you think he's going to cheat on you like Jared did?"

"No, I don't think he would deliberately hurt me," Mia said. "He didn't want the secrecy. That was all my doing. But he has unresolved feelings. I felt it instinctively and he admitted as much. What if he goes back to Katie the way Jared went back to his girlfriend once our marriage lost its appeal?"

"Jared was shallow and self-absorbed," Laney said. "Will isn't like that."

"Maybe not but doesn't my ambivalence confirm that I'm not ready for a man as good as Will?" Mia asked.

"Don't be so hard on yourself. You deserve love and you deserve Will." As Mia left to take Billy home, Laney hugged her again. "Be kind to yourself. Don't let Jared ruin the rest of your life."

Mia didn't feel ambivalent now. Her heart was sore and she longed for Will to hold her and tell her everything was going to be okay, even though it wasn't, even though she'd ruined the best thing that had ever happened to her. She'd taken his good nature and caring for granted and underestimated the depth of his feelings. He'd never been anything but strong and generous and loving and she'd thrown it all away with her lies.

She set aside the green boat and picked up a magenta square, grateful for the therapeutic pastime of patiently folding paper.

The phone rang. Mia reached to answer before it woke Billy. At the sight of Nora's number on caller ID her heart sank. She'd meant to call her mother-in-law earlier. "Hi, Nora. How are you?"

"Fine." Nora sniffed, her voice over-bright. "We missed you at Jared's mass today."

"I was climbing a mountain instead." Mia tucked the phone under her ear, leaving both hands free to make the final intricate fold on the boat. The alpine meadow had been a good call on Will's part, reminding her of the beauty in nature, of the cycles of life, spring following winter. She wished it hadn't been ruined by the ugliness of their argument. And she bitterly regretted hurting him. Hadn't she predicted that, too?

"Mia," Nora began hesitantly. "I called because I wanted to say I'm sorry."

Mia put down the piece of blue paper she'd picked up. "What for?"

Nora's swallow was audible and her voice wavered. "I knew Jared was still seeing his old girlfriend. At one time Jed and I had expected he would marry her. Not that I approved of Jared cheating on you," she added quickly. "But I covered for him. As Jed and I covered for him all his life when he did the wrong thing." Her voice broke. "He was our only child. He was my baby, my beautiful boy."

"I know." Mia felt tears well in her own eyes and laid a gentle hand on Billy, still sleeping peacefully at her side. "You would do anything for your child."

"Please forgive me," Nora said. "Believe me when I say I couldn't have stopped him if I'd tried. He never listened to me. But I shouldn't have lied to you. You deserved better from Jared, and from me."

"I don't hold you responsible." Nora had spoiled Jared as a boy and spared him the consequences of his bad behavior as a man but ultimately Jared was responsible for his own actions. He knew right from wrong and he'd chosen the easy way every time.

"I loved him so much," Nora said, weeping. "For all his faults, I loved my son."

"I loved him, too," Mia said, and it was true. To deny that would mean her marriage had had no value at all. That she'd been a partner in creating her own pain…

Laney's words came back to her. *Be kind to yourself.*

Sudden understanding clicked into place. Pushing away Will was never going to fix anything. All this time she'd been angry with herself for falling for Jared, a charismatic asshole. She'd beaten herself up for being taken in by him. Punished herself by denying herself future happiness. It wasn't her fault. Everyone started out loving Jared until he burned them. She'd been no different. It didn't make her stupid or weak—unless she didn't learn from her experience, that is. Will had taught her what loving a good man could be like. She would be a fool if she didn't grab what he offered with both hands and hang on tight.

But she had to stop hating on Jared, not because he deserved her love but because it was making her suffer to be eaten up inside by regrets and anger. It was time to let all those bad feelings go. She had to if she and Will were to have any chance of happiness.

A kind of peace settled over her. The burden of anger that had weighed her down for over a year seemed to dissolve and seep away.

Nora sniffed, reminding Mia she was still on the phone. "I was wondering…"

"Yes?" Mia said. Was this tentative woman her domineering mother-in-law?

"Would you be able to visit over Easter?" Nora went on quickly. "I promise I won't go overboard on gifts for Jared Jr.—I mean, for Billy. I just want to see him, and you."

"I could probably get a couple of days off," Mia said.

"Oh, thank you," Nora said, tears in her voice. "I was so afraid you would cut us out of our grandson's life."

"I wouldn't do that," Mia said, her conscience pricked. "As long as you understand that I want to raise him my way."

"You're a good mother. You're doing a great job." Nora paused to blow her nose. "D-do you see much of that Will?"

"You mean Billy's godfather? I have been but…" No, she wasn't ready to confide in Nora, nor was Nora ready to hear that Mia was in love again. "I'm not sure how that's going."

"He's a good man," Nora said, surprising her. "He looks out for you."

"I can look out for myself," Mia said.

"True, but it's nice to have someone around who has your back."

"Yes, yes it is." Mia bowed her head and pinched the bridge of her nose as more tears pricked her eyelids. She was surprised to find how much it meant to her for Nora to give her blessing over Will. "I'm so afraid it's too late."

Her phone chimed. It was a text message from Will asking to see her. Hope flared. Quickly she texted back. *Meet me at the lake.*

"Nora, are you still there?" she asked. "Sorry, I've got to go."

DUSK WAS FALLING by the time Will drove into Finley Park. His heart knocking against his chest, he parked next to Mia's red Honda and got out of his truck. She wasn't around so he walked down to the water and looked up and down the shore. The last lingering light of the setting sun turned the

JOAN KILBY

lake to pewter and gold.

"Mia?" he called, cupping his hands around his mouth.

"Will." She emerged from behind a pylon in the shadows of the pier. Billy was flaked out in a pack on her back. Dropping the paper bag she was carrying, she hurried toward him and flung her arms around his neck. "You came."

"Of course I came." He held her tightly, his chest so full he could barely breathe let alone speak. "I'm here. I'll always be here."

"Oh, Will, I'm so sorry." She clung to him, burying her face in his sheepskin jacket. "I screwed up. It wasn't that I didn't trust you, I didn't trust myself. I didn't even realize that until tonight."

"It's okay. We can work things out." He stroked her hair and kissed her temple, rocking her back and forth. "We just need to be honest with each other. And with ourselves."

"I'm so sorry I pushed you away," she mumbled, half sobbing. "I've been so scared, so desperate to protect Billy and myself that I didn't see what was right in front of my face." She lifted her face which was glistening with tears. "I love you. I've never felt like this before with anyone. It's the real thing this time. If you're on the rebound, I'll wait until you're ready. I'll wait forever if necessary."

"You don't need to wait another minute. I love you, too." He kissed Mia's cheeks, her hair, her mouth and eyes. "I'm not on the rebound. I don't love Katie. I was mad at her but I don't even feel that anymore. And I don't want to go out with Shelley or any other woman. The only one I want is you. I'm sorry I wasn't straight about that. I was afraid of scaring you off. I thought if you felt pressured you wouldn't want to spend time with me."

"You were right about that but only because *I* was afraid." Mia searched his eyes for reassurance. "It's not too late for us is it? Can we try again? That's all I care about."

"Now that I've found you, I'm never letting you go," Will said. "We'll be a family—you, me and Billy." At the sound of his name Billy raised his sleepy head from the backpack and smiled when he saw Will. Tears spurted from Will's eyes as he chucked the baby under the chin. "I love you, too, kiddo."

Mia hugged Will tightly. "I'm through with secrets. I want to be your partner openly. I want to walk down the street hand in hand, to kiss you in front of other people, to tell everyone you're Billy's daddy now." She looked up shyly. "If you want to be."

"You bet I do." Will picked her up and swung her, making Billy shriek with laughter. Mia was laughing and crying and so was he. Soon enough, he would tell her in more detail about his epiphanies and hear more of her story. For now he just wanted to hold her and love her and never, ever let her go.

He eased away but kept his arm around her waist as he caught his breath and dashed the moisture from his eyes. "What are you doing down here at the lake?"

"I want to perform a ceremony for Jared." Mia dabbed at her eyes with a tissue. Then she retraced her steps to retrieve the paper bag. "I want to set him free, and to set myself free. Come and help me."

He took her hand and they walked to the water's edge where wavelets lapped at the sand. From the bag Mia removed multicolored boats made of folded paper and set a tea candle in the center of one. Will lit the candle and Mia sent the flickering vessel out into the lake with a gentle push. It wobbled in the rippling water, then steadied and drifted out with the wind.

"I forgive you, Jared," she murmured. "I did love you once. Go in peace."

Will heard her invocation with a full heart. She wouldn't be the passionate woman she was if she hadn't loved the man she'd married, even if Jared had treated her badly.

The next boat she pushed off, she said, "I forgive myself. And I love myself even though I'm not perfect."

No one was perfect, Will knew that much, and certainly he wasn't. He didn't know what Mia needed to forgive herself for but he trusted that in time she would explain fully. From now on there would be no secrets between them. For the worst secret was the one they'd kept from each other—how much they both cared.

A third boat received a burning tea candle. "Nora and Jed, I forgive you." She paused. "Billy loves you because you're his grandparents. I will try to love you too."

Will prepared a fourth boat. Mia shook her head. "That was just a spare."

Still, Will put a candle in the center and placed the boat in the water. "Do you forgive me?"

"There's nothing to forgive." She pushed the candlelit boat out to join the flotilla of tiny flickering flames. It bobbed and almost tipped, then floated serenely.

Then she smiled up at him, her face glowing in the last light of day. "I love you, Will Starr, now and forever."

Epilogue

Christmas Eve…

"GOODNIGHT! MERRY CHRISTMAS," Mia called and waved as she left the big log house. Will carried Billy to the truck.

Linda and Robert stood in their doorway, arms wrapped around each other, bidding Mia and Will farewell after a sumptuous meal. Garret and Cody were staying the night but Alex and Emma and their three-month-old daughter Anya had left a few minutes earlier.

"We should have made more effort with Christmas decorations," Mia said, eyeing the multicolored lights and the Santa's sleigh and reindeer prancing across Will's parents' snow-covered front lawn.

"I've been kind of busy." Will loaded the sleepy one-year-old into the car seat and strapped him in.

"What's up with that, working on Christmas Eve?" Mia complained mildly. Will hadn't accompanied her to Laney and Shelley's open house, instead spending the afternoon at his office, going over accounts that apparently couldn't wait until New Year. She put her hands on the front of his sheepskin jacket and looked up at him, prey to a rare moment of doubt. "You're not…unhappy, are you?" *Like last year?*

"Don't be silly. Since I've been with you and Billy I've never been happier." Will put his arms around her and kissed her nose. Then he pressed his mouth to her lips in a long slow kiss that left her in no doubt about the strength of their relationship. "It was just something I needed to do," he added. "Let's go home."

They got in the truck and headed down the lane that led past the packing shed in a shortcut to Will's house. A few flakes of snow drifted in the headlights. Christmas carols played softly on the radio.

Their house, Mia thought contentedly. She'd given up her apartment as soon as her six-month lease was up and moved in with Will. Together they'd finished decorating and furnishing the home, not following any particular theme, just adding interesting pieces they both loved as they found them.

"Your mom is such a good cook." Mia patted her stomach. "I almost feel as fat as last year at this time when I was pregnant. Remember?"

"How could I forget?" Will smiled. "That night is etched in my memory. The worst and the best night of my life."

"Worst?" Mia said, eyebrows raised.

"Do you have any idea how terrified I was?" Will said.

"Oh, go on. You were a rock." She paused. "Next time you can deliver our baby in the comfort of our own home."

He shot her a glance. "Are you…?"

"No, but I'd like to, in a year or two." Mia reached for his hand and squeezed. "What do you think?"

"Yes, definitely." Will smiled broadly, humming under his breath. Then he broke off as he realized what she'd said. "But no home births. Next time you'll have it in the hospital."

"Let's hope so." Mia glanced into the back seat of the cab. Billy's head with its wavy brown hair lolled, and he clutched his beloved, ragged giraffe with both chubby hands. Speaking of 'best worst'…over his pajamas he wore the garish Christmas sweater Mia had knit for him. By unanimous decision, the Starr family had awarded him first prize in the annual competition. Someday, she was sure, he would beat all the Starr men in the Christmas morning snowshoe race, too.

"He's asleep," she whispered.

"Good, he'll need to rest up for tomorrow. Not many kids have Christmas *and* a birthday." Will glanced at Mia. "I'm glad we left early to have some time to ourselves."

"It's a pretty special night," she agreed and sighed happily. "The night we met. Who'd have thought, when I ran off the road and went into labor that we would end up together?"

They'd married last summer, after the cherry harvest was

A BABY FOR CHRISTMAS

over, in an outdoor ceremony at the winery. In honor of the occasion—and with an eye to future business—the patio had been transformed under Mia's direction into a vine-covered pergola much like that at her uncle's Italian vineyard. Her parents had been there, holding up an iPad on Skype so Mia's grandmother could watch the ceremony. Nora and Jed had attended, too, and after a slight initial awkwardness, had succumbed to the warmth of the Tempestas and of the extended Starr family. Dancing had continued under the stars far into the night.

Over the past year Mia had relinquished some of her cellar door responsibilities to help with the wine making. This year she would also study part time toward her degree. But her wedding aside, the highlight of the year had to be when Will had formally adopted Billy. She'd teased him that now she had to find a new godfather but Will maintained he could fill both roles.

Will slowed as they approached the packing shed, dark but for the strings of colored lights along the roof. Last year they'd been a beacon to her in the storm and possibly saved her and her baby's life, Mia remembered with gratitude.

She also recalled that last Christmas, in a burst of enthusiasm, Will had said he would put up even more lights this year. The flamboyant Italian in her adored over-the-top displays and she'd looked forward to it all year only to be disappointed. Will must have forgotten, or was too busy with work. Since she was hopeless at handyman stuff she hadn't done it. Never mind, Will was so good to her in every other way she could hardly fault him over one small thing.

"Shut your eyes," Will said.

"Why?" Mia asked. Did he think seeing the shed would bring back bad memories for her on Christmas Eve? The car crash, the struggle through the dark and the snow, the scariness of giving birth far from a hospital and doctors? He didn't need to worry. All the bad stuff had faded, eclipsed by the immense joy and overwhelming love she'd experienced since then.

"Just shut them." Will squeezed her knee. "It's a surprise."

Obediently, she closed her eyes, smiling in anticipation. She loved surprises but she was impatient. "When can I open them?"

"A couple more minutes," Will said, as the truck moved faster again, bumping over the packed snow.

It felt like more than a couple of minutes but maybe that was because she was excited. Life with Will wasn't the roller coaster ride of brief highs and horrible lows that she'd been on with Jared. Thank God for that. With Will she found small delights around every corner, sometimes when she least expected it, and in between he provided an even-keeled happiness that gave her, with her more volatile temperament, the emotional security she craved.

"Okay, now," Will said.

Mia opened her eyes and gasped. A blaze of lights illuminated their house. There was a snowman in a sleigh pulled by a polar bear on the lawn. Rows of glowing candy canes lined the driveway. Every tree in the yard was strung with colored lights and reindeer danced along the peaked roof. Lights were strung around every door, window and roofline. But the largest display, in the center of the yard, was a nativity scene with a Madonna in blue and a Joseph looking at a baby in a manger while shepherds and farm animals crowded around.

"Oh my God!" Mia's jaw dropped. "When did you do all this?"

"I've been gathering materials for weeks. Garret and Cody helped me put it up this afternoon," Will said. "That's why I arranged to pick you up from Laney's and go directly to Mom and Dad's or it wouldn't have been a surprise."

Mia felt tears well. She had no words. He'd gone to all this effort just to please her.

"Is it too much?" Will asked. "Too kitschy?"

"There's no such thing as too kitschy." Mia turned to him, her heart full. "It's beautiful. I love it. I love you. Thank you, sweetheart."

"I love you. So much." He pulled her into his arms and she buried her face in his neck.

She was so lucky. Last year at this time she'd hit rock bottom. Now she had Will and Billy and as a bonus, a beautiful home. And if she didn't move she would end up blubbering with happiness all over Will's jacket.

She lifted her face and wiped away her tears and the strands of hair sticking to her cheeks. "Okay, enough of this lovey-dovey stuff. I've got to get out there and take some photos. Wait till my *nonna* sees this. She'll love it."

The End

The Sweet Home Montana series

Book 1: The Secret Son

Book 2: A Baby for Christmas

Available now at your favorite online retailer!

About the Author

Award-winning author Joan Kilby writes sweet, sexy
contemporary romance with a touch of humor. When she's
not working on a new book Joan can often be found at her
local gym doing yoga, or being dragged around the
neighborhood by her Jack "Rascal" terrier. Her hobbies are
growing vegetables, cooking, traveling and reading—not
necessarily in that order. Happily married with three
children, Joan lives in Melbourne, Australia. She loves to
hear from readers so feel free to drop her a line.

Thank you for reading

A Baby for Christmas

If you enjoyed this book, you can find more from all our great authors at TulePublishing.com, or from your favorite online retailer.

TULE
PUBLISHING

Printed in Great Britain
by Amazon

79650251R00144